High Praise for Thomas Wharton's
ICEFIELDS

"Wharton writes with a prose style clear as glacial waters, tempered with brilliant imagery and lucid dialogue. . . . If at times the style betrays Wharton's influences—there are glimpses of Michael Ondaatje, Rudy Wiebe, Gabriel García-Márquez, and Kristjana Gunnars—it is never imitative; Wharton is an original writer and *ICEFIELDS* is an original novel."

—Mark Giles, *Calgary Herald*

"A stunning debut. . . . Wharton's poetic passages betray a slow flame beneath the cool prose, a raw, intense curiosity that fascinates and lays everything bare."

—Joy Gugeler, *Ottawa Citizen*

"This is an uncommonly beautiful novel. . . . Nearly every page gave me something new to marvel at—an image, a gesture, a sudden insight into a character. . . . By the end, I felt that one small, remarkable piece of Canada had been examined with such penetrating eyes that it had begun to glow with hints of universal truth."

—Jack Hodgins

"With its extraordinary setting and engaging blend of fact, myth, and legend, *ICEFIELDS* is a thoroughly enjoyable journey."

—Jenny Gabruch, *Star Phoenix*

"Elegant. . . . Spare and simple, like the glaciers and frozen peaks he describes, Wharton's writing mirrors the beauty of the high alpine landscape. . . . Read this remarkable book."

—R. W. Sandford, *The Jasper Booster*

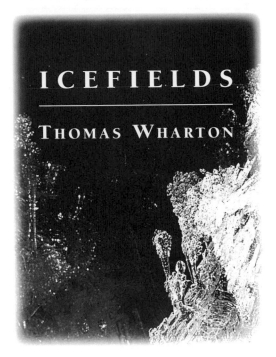

ICEFIELDS

Thomas Wharton

WASHINGTON SQUARE PRESS
PUBLISHED BY POCKET BOOKS

New York   London   Toronto   Sydney   Tokyo   Singapore

This book is a work of fiction. Names, characters, places, and incidents are products of the author's imagination or are used fictiously. Any resemblance to actual events or locales or persons, living or dead, is entirely coincidental.

WSP

A Washington Square Press Publication of
POCKET BOOKS, a division of Simon & Schuster Inc.
1230 Avenue of the Americas, New York, NY 10020

Copyright © 1995 by Thomas Wharton

Published by arrangement with NeWest Press

All rights reserved, including the right to reproduce this book or portions thereof in any form whatsoever. For information address NeWest Press, c/o Stoddart Publishing, Suite 310, 10359-82 Avenue, Edmonton, Alberta, Canada T6E 1Z9

ISBN: 0-671-00220-1

First Washington Square Press trade paperback printing October 1996

10 9 8 7 6 5 4 3 2 1

WASHINGTON SQUARE PRESS and colophon are registered trademarks of Simon & Schuster Inc.

Cover design by Brigid Pearson
Front cover photo by Tommy Flynn/Photonica
Interior photo credits: pp. iii and vii, Alberta Environmental Protection National Resources Service; p. ix, Ernest Brown Collection (B9822) Provincial Archives of Alberta; pp. 1, 61, 139, 185, and 224, Public Affairs Bureau Collection (PA 225/2)

Printed in the U.S.A.

FOR MY FAMILY

AS IF EVERYTHING IN THE WORLD

IS THE HISTORY OF ICE.

✳

Michael Ondaatje

COMING THROUGH SLAUGHTER

A NOTE TO THE READER

*This book is a work of fiction and as such
contains deliberate historical and geographical
inaccuracies. The characters, places, and events
depicted are products of the author's imagination or are used in a fictional context. Any
resemblance to actual events, locales, persons, or
glaciers, living or dead, is entirely coincidental.*

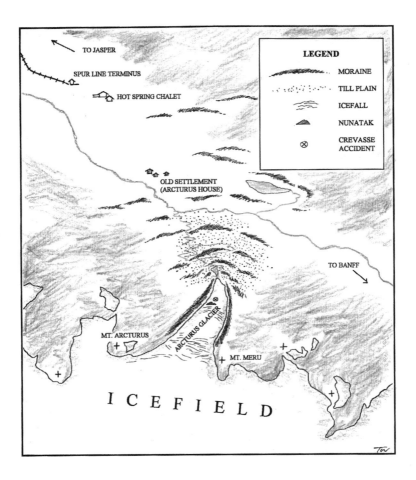

TO JASPER

SPUR LINE TERMINUS

HOT SPRING CHALET

OLD SETTLEMENT
(ARCTURUS HOUSE)

TO BANFF

MT. ARCTURUS

ARCTURUS GLACIER

MT. MERU

I C E F I E L D

LEGEND

MORAINE

TILL PLAIN

ICEFALL

NUNATAK

CREVASSE
ACCIDENT

NÉVÉ

THIS HIGH PLAIN OF SNOW AND ICE FROM WHICH THE

GLACIERS DESCEND CANNOT BE SEEN FROM THE VALLEY.

IT MUST BE IMAGINED.

1

At a quarter past three in the afternoon, on August 17, 1898, Doctor Edward Byrne slipped on the ice of Arcturus glacier in the Canadian Rockies and slid into a crevasse.

Frank Trask, the expedition guide, was the first to notice his disappearance. He paused in his slow trudge to make a head count and saw, against the glare of the ice, one less dark, toiling figure than there had been moments before. Trask called out to the others walking farther ahead on the glacier. They turned at his shout and descended quickly to where he stood.

On this bare, windswept slope of ice there was only one place Byrne could be. The climbing party crouched at the edge of the chasm where the young doctor's snow goggles lay, the strap caught on a projecting spine of ice. They shouted his name down into the darkness, but heard nothing. Trask unwound the coil of rope from over his shoulder and knotted a stirrup in one end.

—I'm not married, Professor Collie said. I'll go.

Trask shook his head.

—I am, he said. I will.

There was no time to argue. One end of the rope was secured around a rough bollard hacked out of the ice, and Trask tied the other around his chest. Slipping his foot into the stirrup, he took hold of the rope and stepped backwards into the abyss.

In blue-black darkness almost sixty feet below the surface, his gloved hand touched the doctor's boot. He realized Byrne was wedged upside down between the narrowing crevasse walls. Trask spoke his name and nudged him cautiously with his knee, but Byrne did not respond. The only sound was the muffled splash of meltwater. Trask shouted up to the others and after a few moments a second rope snaked down towards him from above. He caught the end of the rope and hung in space, waiting for his eyes to grow accustomed to the deep blue gloom. After a few moments he could see that the rucksack on Byrne's back was jammed against an outcrop of the ice wall. This lucky chance had saved him from falling even further, but now the rucksack would only be a hindrance to the rescue.

Trask squirmed himself down into the narrow space beside Byrne. With his hunting knife he sliced through one shoulder strap, then worked the free end of the rope behind the doctor's back, grasped it with the fingers of his other hand and slowly tugged it around. The doctor did not move. Trask let out a long breath. He felt sweat cooling on his neck.

When the rope was snug and knotted under Byrne's arms, Trask cut the other strap and gave the rucksack a shove with his boot. It tumbled down into the dark with a muffled clang of metal.

What the hell was he carrying in there?

Byrne began to slide downward, but the rope went taut and held him.

—I've got him, Trask shouted. Pull him up, slowly.

Byrne, and then Trask, were hauled to the surface. The doctor's skin was pale blue, his beard and clothing covered in a lacquer of refrozen meltwater.

Professor Collie knelt and examined him,

unwound the ice-encrusted scarf from around Byrne's neck and felt for a pulse.

—He's alive. Unconscious.

With his teeth Trask pulled off his soaked gloves and spat them onto the ice.

—Then he missed all the fancy words I used trying to get that damn rope around him.

—Hypothermia, said Professor Collie. We have to get him warmed up.

The four men carried Byrne down the long, sloping tongue of the glacier to the terminus, where the wranglers were camped, waiting with the horses. Nigel the cook saw them coming and had a fire started and tea brewing when they arrived. Stripped of his soaked, stiffened clothing and bundled in a wool blanket, Byrne was propped upright in front of the fire. Drooping forward, he made a barely audible sound, a gasping hiccup. The professor rubbed his limbs and chest.

—The pulse is weak, but he's still with us.

Byrne shuddered and moved his arms. His breathing became audible. A pink glow spread slowly from the center of his chest, outward to the limbs, suffusing the blue pallor. He yawned, opened his eyes, and shut them again.

The professor forced hot tea down Byrne's throat.

—We must get him away from the ice, Collie said. I'm afraid that if we bivouac here he might relapse.

As he spoke, he pried the pocketwatch from Byrne's closed fist.

2

Dark was rising in the valley and, with it, a liquid chill to the air. Collie intended to make camp in the shelter of the nearest stand of trees, where there would be some cover from the freezing wind off the glacier. He stood up from his ministrations over the doctor and glanced around.

—Where is Trask?

—He thought he saw lights, Thompson said, further down the valley. He went to have a look.

After a few minutes, Trask rode up.

—I've got us some shelter.

He had found people living at the site of the old Arcturus trading post, just a short ride away. He told the settlers about Byrne, and they would have blankets and hot food ready when the expedition arrived.

Trask was astounded at his own discovery.

—I thought the place had been abandoned years ago.

The wranglers improvised a sling with a blanket and willow poles and carried Byrne while the others rode. Trask led them through the stunted trees along the edge of the creek into a grassy clearing. They saw lighted windows in the darkness and headed toward them.

—Dear God, Stutfield said. To think people live here through the winter for the sake of a few marten skins.

A woman stood at the door of the nearest cabin, holding up an oil lamp. She beckoned them inside.

3

Byrne dreamed of flowers.

He breathed their scents and read the names that ran in orderly columns down the pages of his botanical notebook. Names of the flowers he had been collecting. The seeds and bulbs he had stored with their native earth in the tin specimen box he carried in his rucksack. He walked among them, he breathed and named, not knowing or caring if the scents matched the names he gave them. Flowers of snow melt, of early and full summer, of dry August.

Western Anemone, or Chalice Flower. Glacier Lily. Wild Blue Flax. Four species of violet, three of *Orchidaceae*.

Flowers of the lush valleys and the high, windscoured slopes.

Yellow Mountain Avens. Bluebell, *hedysarum*. River Beauty and Grass of Parnassus. Indian Paintbrush.

He woke in a log cabin, on a bed, under soft blankets of fur. Looking up at smoke-grimed rafters, the glitter of melting frost on the wood. His arm was stiff, held tightly against his chest with a cloth or bandage. He moved, and was aware of his nakedness under the thick fur blankets.

He lifted his head and looked around at sagging shelves cluttered with tins, bottles, books. Skins and sleek pelts hung from the walls between the shelves. A pot-bellied stove stood in one corner. There were three small windows, two of them on one wall papered over with oil-stained parchment.

Framed in the open doorway, a meadow of flowering grass. In a chair by the door sat a woman, reading.

She heard him move and glanced up.

—The flowers, Byrne said. In my rucksack.

—Lost, the woman said. The guide had no choice. He couldn't free you without cutting away your kit. Don't try to sit up. Your collarbone.

Byrne lay back on the furs.

—You'll have to stay here for a while, the woman said.

—Where am I?

—This is Jasper.

His fall.

They had unroped minutes before, at Professor Collie's insistence. The ice was bare of snow and unsafe for roped travel: one man's mishap would bring the others down with him. The guide had argued with him over that decision, but Collie's word was final. Trask had been hired in Banff to lead the expedition as far as his knowledge of the terrain surpassed the professor's, and to him the glacier was unknown territory. This was Collie's domain.

Once free of the rope, they started up through the labyrinth of crevasses and snowbridges at the base of the first icefall.

They skirted the edge of a narrow chasm. Byrne stepped up close, intrigued by the rippled bands of ice along the rim of the crevasse. Frozen waves. A faint childhood memory came to him, a fairy-tale sea from one of his mother's stories. There had been a picture of waves like this in the book she read to him in bed at night. He took off his green-tinted snow goggles for a better look. The ice was aquamarine, deepening further down to blue-black.

He looked up, glanced around. Collie and the others were already well ahead of him. And Trask was several yards behind, taking slow, careful steps, his head down.

Byrne inched closer to the crevasse. He knew it was foolish even as he did it, but the wet cold seemed to have numbed his good sense along with his fingers and toes. Planting one foot behind him, he slid the other cautiously to the edge. He leaned forward, extended his arms for balance like a man on a high wire. He bent from the waist, craning his neck, and then his forward leg gave way.

He could not remember falling, but suddenly he was in darkness, meltwater splattering over him. He felt icy rivulets of water slide upward from his neck to his face and into his hair, and after a dazed moment he realized he was hanging upside down.

He felt no pain, not in those first moments. Distant shouts reached him from above, but when he tried to answer, the ice wall slapped his voice back at him, flat and dead.

6

The woman was gone. He was alone in the cabin. He drifted between sleep and wakefulness, jolted awake often by his arms or legs jerking, as if to ward off a blow or escape some unseen danger. In these moments it seemed to him that the different regions of his body lay at an immense distance from one another.

He remembered the woman saying she would

fetch Collie and the others. He was confused by this, thinking that they were still on the glacier and that she would have to climb up after them. Then her words came back to him. *This is Jasper.* He was in a cabin. They had carried him off the ice and brought him to this place.

He closed his eyes and remembered the dead gloom of the crevasse. And then the ice creaking and groaning as it flooded slowly with light.

7

He knew that the sun must have broken through the swath of cloud hanging over the glacier. Somehow its light had found a way into the depths of the crevasse. The ice wall in front of him became lit with a pale blue-green radiance.

At first he felt only anger, at himself and the others. Far above him, Professor Collie, Stutfield, Thompson, Trask, would be welcoming the sunshine while it lasted, unwinding the scarves from around their necks, taking off their thick gloves, glorying in that sudden benediction of light. A rest from the dull overcast sky and the stinging crystalline shards streaming off the névé. And while they sunned themselves he was trapped here because of his own stupidity, upside down, freezing to death.

He struggled to move, to turn his head and shout upward. Still he felt no pain. Nothing, and then horror. *I've broken my neck.*

He moved his arm. His legs. They still obeyed him. It was the cold that was numbing him, and the shock of his fall. His spine was not broken. The others would find him. They would free him, and he would have a wonder to report to Collie. *A hitherto unknown periscopic property of glacial ice.*

He stared straight ahead and realized he could see quite far into the ice. It was almost free of impurities, like a wall of furrowed, tinted glass. He squinted. There was something in the ice, a shape, its outline sharpening as the light grew. A fused mass of trapped air bubbles, or a vein of snow, had formed a chance design, a white form embedded within the darker ice and revealed by the light of the sun.

A pale human figure, with wings.

The white figure lay on its side, the head turned away from him. Its huge wings were spread wide, one of them cracked obliquely near the tip, the broken pinions slightly detached.

One arm was also visible, outstretched, in the semblance of some gesture that Byrne felt he had seen before, but could not interpret. A remembered sculpture, or one of Blake's hovering, pitying spirits.

The shape gleamed wetly, like fine porcelain or delicately veined marble.

Byrne groped for his notebook but found he could not reach around to the side pocket of his rucksack. His other arm was stuck fast, dead. He struggled, gasping against the pressure on his chest that would not allow him to fill his lungs. Pain awoke, tearing through his neck and shoulder.

I'm alive.

He held himself still, clamped his jaw against a rising scream. He was suddenly aware that any movement could send him plummeting deeper into the crevasse.

8

He was thirsty.

He scraped at the ice wall with his one free hand, pressed his fingers to it until he felt them burn, then held them in his mouth.

His head and chest pounded with a dull throb of pain that he realized was his own heartbeat. He had to think, keep his mind working and alert. What would the orientation of this artifact be if he were not looking at it upside down? Had it fallen from above? Or seeped in from below? Did the ice encasing it cause a magnifying effect? It seemed to be very large. Large enough, if it suddenly stirred to life and flowed toward him through the ice, to surround and enfold him with its wings.

He closed his eyes. When he looked again, the light had faded. The ice wall was blank.

He laughed. It was absurd. A magnificent, impossible figure from a long-forgotten childhood dream.

9

How long have I been here?

Minutes, or hours. There was no way to tell. The pain had sunk and contracted into a jagged stone in the middle of his chest. When he moved his jaw he heard the skin of ice on his neck cracking. He argued with himself, reasoning against the desire to sleep, against the insane thought that he had been wedged in this crevasse for centuries. Freezing into absolute stillness, his thoughts crystallized around one idea. He moved an arm, fumbled at his coat for his pocket watch.

He had to know the time.

Time was the one constant. It did not change or freeze into immobility. Time would go on and so would he.

Do I have the watch in my hand? He could not be sure. His fingers were numb.

Perhaps it did not matter. He closed his eyes.

Her name was Sara.

She fed Byrne spoonfuls of broth from a pot of mulligatawny stew. Since he had first awakened, his tongue and throat had been burning, while the rest of his body shivered. The spicy broth was painful to swallow, but after a few mouthfuls Byrne felt warmth growing in him. He looked more closely at the woman.

She was dark-skinned, her face thin, the cheekbones sharp. Her long graying hair was tied back at the nape of the neck with an ancient strip of leather. She had on a woollen coat over what looked, to Byrne's puzzlement, like a sari of dark green cloth wrapped tightly around her. At her neck he glimpsed a brooch, a swan on a blue enamel field.

In the light from the doorway, her skin shone like a young woman's. Age was in her grey eyes, in the measured steps she took from the stove to his bedside.

She turned away from him to set the soup pot on the table, and he saw his grandmother. Nana. He was lying on a cot in her kitchen, under a thick wool blanket, feverish, sick. Outside, in the garden, a soft rain falling. With tongs, Nana banked the smoking clumps of turf around the huge iron pot in the fireplace. She was baking bread, singing to him as she worked. Soothing him.

The woman named Sara moved quietly to the doorway.

—Your friends are outside. I'll tell them you're awake.

When she had spoken again, he identified at last the faint remnants of an Anglo-Indian accent.

Byrne felt he should talk to her, but he had no idea what words to say. She went out, closing the door behind her. He lay back on the bed and closed his eyes.

11

When he woke again fragments of the last few hours came back to him. Bright pain slicing through the fog of delirium as Collie tended to his broken collarbone. The maddening weakness of his limbs when he moved to the edge of the bed, slid his legs out from under the blankets and tried to stand. He wanted to show Collie he was capable of going with them, at least back to the base camp if no farther. But Collie would not listen. They debated carrying him back down the trail to Banff. There was no way to get a stretcher over the pass. The rivers would be swollen now with late summer meltwater, dangerous even for able-bodied travellers. He imagined at times that he was still in the crevasse, listening to their talk from a great depth.

Furious at them, at himself, he shouted at Collie and fell back on the bed, exhausted.

They had left him in the care of the woman, to make one more attempt to locate the mountain Collie was searching for. *This time we'll scale the peak that flanks the glacier,* Collie had said, *rather than venture onto the ice again. It should give us a better view of the surrounding terrain. We'll see what we can see from up there, and then we'll come back for you.*

Byrne kept silent and then Collie added, *You'll be well looked after here.*

When they returned he would be transported east to Edmonton in a pony cart. Driven by a man named Swift, an American who lived further down the Athabasca valley.

Lying alone in the silent cabin, he decided this plan was right. It was what he would agree to if one of the others had been injured. A part of the unwritten code he had accepted by joining an expedition of the Royal Geographical Society.

He would lie here and rest.

He slept.

12

Drifting back to England in his dreams.

The memory of visits to the botanical gardens

at Kew, out of the city haze and into a fragrant, tidy wilderness. Marvelling at flowers grown from the specimens collected by David Douglas and other early scientist-explorers of the Rockies. In the humid glass cathedral of the Alpine House he leaned forward and breathed their delicate scents.

He took a young woman to the gardens one day. Martha Croston. It was the day he almost proposed to her.

They were there now, weren't they? Opening his eyes upon the long, well-tended rows of plants, he would take her arm, stroll among the flowers, inhaling their mingled odours, watch with a rare feeling of envy as the old whiskered nurseryman carried his trays of seedlings reverently down the aisle.

He opened his eyes. The woman's face leaning over him.

—You are beautiful, he said.

Her grey eyes looked into his for a long moment and then she moved away.

13

It was at Kew where he first met Professor Collie and learned of his proposed expedition. Collie amazed him: a chemist, a pioneer of colour photography, an artist. Mountaineering was only one of his many passions.

The goal is Mount Brown, Collie had said. *Find it, or prove it a hoax. It's been on every map in the empire for sixty years as the highest on this continent. And no one even knows if it really exists. So far no one has thought to go and verify the one lone sighting that got it on the maps in the first place.*

He was determined to rediscover the lost giant and, if possible, to be the first to reach its summit.

Among the flowers at Kew, putting himself forward as a candidate for expedition doctor, Byrne formed his own unstated plan: to create a private botanical collection when he returned to London, grown from the field specimens he would gather during the search for Collie's lost mountain. Perhaps one day he would even see some of his own flowers blossoming here along the lofty aisles at Kew.

And when he returned he would also ask Martha to be his wife.

14

He thought about climbing back down into the crevasse and searching for his rucksack, the tin plant collection box it carried. Salvaging what he could of his specimens. Of course Collie would not allow it and, even if he did, by now the narrow chasm into which he had fallen had probably changed shape, or closed over altogether as the glacier crept relentlessly forward.

Then he remembered what he had seen in the ice wall.

15

During the daytime children gathered at the open doorway of the old trading post to stare at Byrne. Women came and herded them away and turned their heads to look at him themselves. He also saw, or thought he saw as he drifted between wakefulness and dreams, the dark shapes of men in the clearing, men leading horses, followed by dogs, men with bundles on their backs.

Only Sara came near him, and she said almost nothing.

16

A noise, a distant rapping on glass. Someone knocking. Brought him up out of sleep to answer the call. Always urgent at this hour.

He sat up. There in the cabin window, a giant's hand, fingers outstretched, knocking against the glass.

He made a sound of sleepy terror. *Hahhh.*

The hand bobbed stiffly, as if carved of wood, and then sank below the window frame. Elk antler.

He took a deep breath, the nightmare fears of childhood subsiding. The fur blanket slid from his shoulder. He leaned on his good arm and listened while the huge animal bumped along the wall of the cabin, foraging the long grass.

Then he saw Sara in the doorway.

—I heard you cry out, she said.

Byrne shook his head.

—It was nothing. The elk, it woke me up rather suddenly.

—He comes here to rub the velvet off his antlers. It's the rutting season.

—Ah.

—Do you need anything? I'll get the fire going.

Outside, the sky was grey. Not yet sunrise. He wondered if Sara ever slept. Watching her gather up an armful of kindling for the stove, he suddenly knew that she was young, not many years his elder. He had been fooled by a stillness within her movements that suggested age, but was in fact her body's own quiet grace.

—No, nothing. Well, yes, now that I'm awake, I'd like some tea.

She turned toward the stove.

—Wait, he said. One moment.

He looked closely at her.

—Tell me about this place.

He would say nothing about what he had seen in the crevasse, give nothing away. Only listen.

17

She told him that this small cabin was once a Hudson's Bay Company trading post. Snow House. Sara's father, Viraj, took it over when the trader before him left to try his luck goldpanning in the Cariboo. There had been no traffic in furs through this valley for years, and it was her cabin now. While Byrne slept here she was staying with her nearest neighbours.

Before her father settled in the valley and took over the trading post, he had been a valet in the service of an Englishman, Lord Sexsmith.

During his travels through Rajasthan, Sexsmith had taken Viraj on to care for the horses. He was pleased with the young man's quiet efficiency and, when he left India and returned to England, Viraj remained in his entourage.

—Sexsmith was not a healthy man, Sara told Byrne. Lung trouble. His doctor thought a less damp and foggy climate would help. Someplace higher up, colder. He looked through an atlas and chose the Rockies. Of course my father had little choice but to go with him.

Byrne sat propped up in the narrow bed. She talked while she made tea and hot cakes for him and sat with him and talked while he ate.

—My father was sick at heart when he first came to this country. He had a premonition that he would die here, far from his own country, among strangers.

Byrne stared into his teacup, swirled the cold dregs. He was alone here, with this youthful ancient woman. A woman with stories.

18

—They were on the plain of stumps outside Fort Edmonton, Sara said. Sexsmith was on his favourite horse, a black gelding he had named The Night. My father was holding the reins. They were starting that morning for the mountains, with an escort of Company men. Sexsmith stretched out his arms and said

The prisoner of civilization is free.

19

Sexsmith had been forewarned about the mosquitoes. He paid no attention to the stories. Frontier exaggeration.

When the sun went down, however, they came. The stars were blotted out by them. The Company men had gathered loads of dry wood as they travelled during the day, and at night they lit smudge fires in a ring around the camp, to keep the tormented horses from stampeding.

Baptiste the Iroquois showed Viraj how to crush alder leaves and rub the pulp on the bites to soothe them.

Sexsmith had his tent cocooned in layers of fine netting. He took refuge there, his face and arms covered in a salve of camphor ice, to read Shakespeare.

A thunderstorm one evening gave a respite from the buzzing plague. At dawn the next day several of the horses wandered away from camp and rolled in a wet buffalo wallow at the side of the trail. They had to be ridden or loaded with baggage as they were, encased in carapaces of dried mud. Terrible saddle sores appeared on their flanks and were rubbed with salt to form calluses. Three of the ponies could no longer carry packs and had to be turned loose.

One morning as the camp was being struck, a party of Cree hunters appeared on a hill and rode slowly toward them. Sexsmith put a hand on the rifle sheathed at his side, when a glad shout of recognition erupted from one of his men.

The Cree hunters said they had heard of Sexsmith's expedition and had come with a gift of bear tongues for the great chief visiting their lands. Macpherson bartered with them for horses. To make the trade, Sexsmith was forced to surrender half the tobacco he had brought.

Sexsmith also solemnly accepted a buffalo cap and cloak from the hunters. Later that day he gave them to Viraj.

I'm afraid I would make a laughable figure in these hides.

20

Two visions drew the English lord on into the mountains.

The first was a grizzly bear, thundering across a meadow toward him. He would be kneeling with Macpherson, rifles leveled, rock steady. Macpherson, with eyes so sharp the other men said he could see stars in daylight. The flash and report, and after a heartbeat the great bear toppling, a mountain of silver fur and muscle avalanching into the dust. Baptiste would cut out the grizzly's heart, present it to him. He dreamed of the hot sensual heart sliding into his palm.

The second vision was the Grail.

—You are Irish, I think, Sara said to Byrne. She sat on a pine chair in the doorway of the cabin, smoking a pipe. The watery light of dusk reflected in her grey eyes.

—I was born in Dublin, Byrne nodded, frowning. He turned in the bed, glanced away toward the window. But I've lived in England since I was eleven.

Sara smiled.

—I thought I could hear it in your voice. You asked for another cup of tay. My father used to mimic the accent. *Jaysus Mary and Joseph*. It would send the traders into laughing fits.

Byrne pushed away the memory of a dark church niche, dim candlelight. A sad, gentle face of cold stone. Ever this day be at my side.

—My father was a doctor, Byrne said. He practiced in London for several years before his marriage. When my mother died we went to live there.

He sipped his tea and waited for her to speak.

—They made fun of my father, Sara finally said. The Company men. They called him the tarred butler, the black man. Even though like many of them he was a half-caste in his own country. His father was an Englishman.

They struggled up the gorge of a river just that day named by Sexsmith. Hemmed in by wet, overhanging walls of rock, deafened by the roar of rapids.

The fur trade trail took them high above the river, then vanished in a steep escarpment of broken slate at the foot of a cliff. The horses shied and stumbled. Sexsmith climbed down from the saddle. Viraj led the nervous horse while Sexsmith lit his pipe and lagged behind, smoking and picking his way slowly across the loose scree.

Like walking on a church roof, Sexsmith shouted to Viraj. *Albeit one badly in need of repair.*

The Company men often sang songs as they traveled, but now they were silent. They worked their way across the clinking, clattering slate like sleepwalkers, like knights bewitched by music from under the earth. Only when a horse strayed out of line was the quiet disturbed, by an echoing curse.

Demon. Old sinner. Tonight I'll wear your hide for a blanket.

Each man was absorbed in his own efforts to keep a straight heading, to step forward without sinking sideways into the deepening bed of slate. After a while the tight column of horses and men broke apart, meandering at a tortuous pace across the scree.

Sexsmith tapped his finished pipe against a

rock. He looked up to find himself several metres down-slope from the rest of the party. He had been smoking and musing on Caliban's beautiful speech in the third act of *The Tempest*, the rhythms of which had become strangely mixed up with the *chink clunk* of slate under his boots.

Sexsmith shook his head and began to climb upward, only to find that after a full day's march, this kind of effort was beyond him. The sun had heated the dull, flat shards of rock into kiln bricks. Sexsmith wiped his brow and his hand came away dripping with sweat. With effort he set down a booted foot, felt it slide helplessly underneath him, sending a cascade of shards down the slope. He cursed. Plunging forward, he stumbled to his hands and knees, scrambled for purchase. He was sinking into rock, drowning.

Viraj. Help me.

23

Viraj heard the shout and turned. Through a liquid shimmer of heat he saw Sexsmith's flailing arms. He dropped the horse's reins and took a few steps down the slope. The scree gave way beneath him, throwing him off balance. He leapt forward to keep from falling, and broke into a run, taking great bounding strides, each footfall plunging down, pushing up a mound of rock and springing free.

A smile spread across his face. He was moving with the element now, not against it. Leaping like a gazelle, the fringes of his buffalo cap fluttering as he descended.

Like feather'd Mercury, the lines came to Sexsmith haltingly, as he watched Viraj's descent. *Vaulting with such ease.*

24

Above the canyon wall, a snowy peak rose into view, the pyramid of a mountain they had seen the day before from a distance and remarked on for its beauty.

A palace, Sexsmith had written in his journal the night before, *rose-pearl in the late sunlight, an Asiatic temple floating in air.*

This close the mountain was a massive presence. Sexsmith closed his eyes, overcome by sudden vertigo. Here was the edge of the earth, and far below it clouds drifted over an empty blue ocean. He took a deep shuddering breath. His body went slack and he dropped the reins.

Viraj, your arm.

Sexsmith crawled down from the saddle and staggered forward. He took the spyglass from around his neck with trembling fingers, sank to one knee.

He was thirty-one years old. A Victorian in the presence of the sublime.

25

Sara took Byrne with her on this journey that she had not witnessed, that for all he knew she might have been weaving out of thin mountain air. A mythology of cast-off stories, poetry, scraps of historical fact, growing and changing shape like whorls of smoke in the gloom of a snow-locked cabin. What he learned of her life was gathered in the shadow of her father's story.

She lived alone in her cabin, in the midst of this Métis settlement. The Stoney people she had known as a child no longer wintered in the Athabasca territory. With the signing of the treaties they had chosen land further south.

Viraj, her father, was dead. Just as he had feared on the day Sexsmith stabbed a finger at that blank, wordless space in the atlas, he had journeyed here and never left.

On the morning of the fourth day, Byrne insisted he was strong enough to leave the bed. He kept himself covered with the fur blanket while Sara handed him the clothes and personal effects that Collie had left with her. She went outside to wait, at his request, while he struggled into his shirt, trousers, and boots. When he had dressed she came back in with a fur robe, placed it over his shoulders, helped him out onto the stoop of the cabin.

This place that Sara called Jasper was a gathering of log cabins and plank shacks, ranged over a grassy river flat. Above each roof stood a thin rope of smoke. There was no one about. A sandy-coloured dog, stretched out on the porch of the nearest cabin, raised its head and watched Byrne for a moment, then went back to sleep. At the far end of the meadow a few untethered horses were moving among the trees, lowering their dark heads to the grass.

Byrne shivered and tugged the robe closer around him.

Above the dark slope of the valley rose the mountains. Byrne raised a hand to shade his eyes, grown accustomed to the cabin's cave-like gloom, against their painful brilliance. For a moment he could not believe in these hard, unfathomable masses of rock. They seemed to hang suspended in the sky. A quick, cold breath might shatter them like an illusion of ice crystals and light.

Squinting, he picked out the crevasses and icefalls of Arcturus glacier. From this distance they seemed only delicate, spidery wrinkles in pale blue silk. Above them gleamed the white rim of the névé,

where the glacier spilled from a gap between the flank-
ing peaks. A slender curve of burning snow.

If all had gone well on the second attempt,
Professor Collie and the others would be up there,
beyond that shining edge.

—There are no doctors here, Sara said. They
say the railroad will be coming this way in a few years.
The workers will need a doctor to travel up and down
the line. You could be stationed here.

Byrne shook his head.

—My life is in England.

26

After two days Swift had not yet come to meet Byrne.

—He visits us once a year, Sara said. He buys
furs and dried meat to see him through the winter. He
says he's too busy with his crops and his inventions to
bother with hunting.

—Inventions?

—He wants to grind his own flour, so he's
building a sluice and a water-wheel.

Lucas Napoleon Swift, from Saint Louis. At seventeen he was a bugler in General Custer's cavalry.
Then he came down with cholera and was sent home,
two weeks before Little Bighorn.

—He roamed around after that, Sara said,

always afraid the death he'd cheated was coming for him. He didn't want anyone else nearby when it found him.

Twenty-five years after Sexsmith's journey, Swift arrived in the valley of the Athabasca, one of the very few white men to make an appearance during all that time. The fur trade had gradually died out and there was no longer any material reason to follow the old overland trail. Until men like Swift came looking for the one precious substance that remained here: the gold of solitude and silence.

Sara sat down by the bedside, opened a book. Motes of dry paper fell from its foxed pages and flickered in the slanting light.

—Sexsmith liked to have my father read poetry to him. And when I was a girl my father read it to me.

She turned the pages slowly, searching, and then began to read aloud. In a voice like spring leaves against a windowpane.

> In Xanadu did Kubla Khan
> A stately pleasure-dome decree:
> Where Alph, the sacred river, ran
> Through caverns measureless to man
> Down to a sunless sea.

She read the poem to the end and then asked him if he wanted her to keep reading.

—I want to hear more about Sexsmith's expedition, he said.

She got up and set the book back in its place on the shelf, and when she turned to him again she was smiling.

27

Viraj prepared a bath for the lord.

On the advice of the outfitter at Fort Edmonton, excess baggage had been left behind. But his collapsible India rubber bathtub was one of the few luxuries Sexsmith could not part with. He allowed no one else the use of it. Here, immersed in water heated over the campfire, he read Shakespeare and made critical notes in the margins, the book propped on a split log laid across the tub's rim.

Perfect, Sexsmith sighed as he eased himself into the sagging tub. He smiled at Viraj, who stood waiting at the door of the tent. *Exactly the temperature and humidity of your monsoon season.*

One evening when the bath had just been made ready, Viraj informed his lordship that a group of Stoney hunters was camped on the far shore of the river. Some of the hunters had come across to meet with the Company men. Among them were two brothers who claimed they had travelled much in the country that lay ahead.

Send for them, Sexsmith said, turning a page with the ragged end of his quill pen.

He was still soaking when the Stoney brothers, Joseph and Elias, entered the tent unannounced, Viraj gesturing them away in alarm. They looked blankly at Sexsmith and then their faces softened into shy smiles. Viraj coughed, and Sexsmith glanced up over his Shakespeare. He gave a quick snort of amusement.

Can you speak English? he asked them. They nodded. Sexsmith waved Viraj out. *Leave them be. There's no need for the usual proprieties.*

28

The brothers returned the next day, with a young woman. A thin robe of ermine fur covered her shoulders. Her face was painted blue. The Company men watched silently as she walked through the camp with the Stoney brothers. The passage of an unknown animal.

Except for the robe, she was dressed like the brothers and her hair was tied back. Viraj at first thought she was a young man. And then, as she passed the place where he was standing, she turned, her eyes darting white amid the dark blue face paint.

Wapamathe, Baptiste said. *The throat cutters.*

And the girl is goddamned windigo for sure, someone else whispered in mock terror to Viraj. *She'll devour you in the night.*

The brothers met with Sexsmith in a spruce bark tipi at the edge of camp. Joseph said she was their adopted sister. She knew the land better than they did because her people had once lived here in this valley, and even deeper in the mountains. They called her Athabasca.

She is one of the Snake people, Joseph said. *Maybe the last one. A healer.*

On this trip, he told Sexsmith, she could gather herbs needed for her medicines.

She will keep her magic potions to herself, Sexsmith said. He lifted a paper cone in his finger tips, held it up before Joseph and Elias who sat across from him in the circle of men.

He bit on the end of the small white cone, pulled it quickly away from his mouth as the paper fussed into blue flame. The brothers blinked and Joseph jerked his head away as Sexsmith thrust the sputtering fire towards him.

The tipi filled with laughter. Sexsmith smiled and set the tiny flame to the end of his pipe.

The humble Prometheus match, he said. The young woman sat staring into the fire pit. Sexsmith frowned.

Are you aught that man may question?

She did not move. Sexsmith turned to Joseph.

Does she speak English? I would like to know how she can find her way so unerringly if she never looks up.

Joseph said something to her in a language punctuated with quick hand movements. She raised her head. The flat stone hanging from a leather strap around her neck caught the firelight and gleamed.

The young woman held out her left hand, the open palm toward Sexsmith.

She has the tracks of the rivers, Joseph said. *On her hand. The rivers and all the streams.*

Sexsmith leaned forward and looked closely at the young woman's hand. He stabbed a finger into her palm.

What's this reddish blotch?

Their enemies came, killed them all, Joseph said. *She ran and fell on the cooking stones.* He pointed to her pendant. *This one she kept in her hand.*

An incomplete map, then, Sexsmith said. *But I imagine there are a few gold-seekers,* he sawed at his wrist with his pipe stem, *who would do anything to get it.*

29

At night the temperature in Jasper plummeted. A solemn young man Byrne had not seen before came in, carrying an armload of firewood.

—Thank you, Byrne said.

The young man set the wood down by the stove and went out again without a word.

With his good arm Byrne dragged the pine chair closer to the stove. He huddled there, humming to himself, bored, uncomfortable. As the wood burned down in the belly of the stove it collapsed on itself with soft hisses and thumps. The only sounds, until Byrne thought he heard music.

Drums, pipes, a fiddle. Bursts of laughter.

He got up from the chair. The glass-paned window was frosted over. He breathed on the glass, rubbed it with his sleeve, and peered out. A tiny square of gold light hung in the blackness. The window of a nearby cabin, shadows flickering within it.

While Byrne watched, the frost invaded the clear patch of glass he was looking through. The distant square of light dilated into a constellation of gold points.

St. Agnes' Eve—Ah, bitter chill it was!

That damned poetry.

Dropping back into the chair, he was enveloped again in a sphere of warmth that extended just to the reach of his arm. He discovered the boundary of this shell by breathing out, watching the exhaled air appear, a cloud of steam that congealed and slid to the floor. When he rocked back too far, he felt the hairs on the back of his neck rising as they passed through the sphere and into cold air.

He waited out the night, reaching for sticks of wood and tossing them on the fire.

30

—They forded the river at sunset, Sara told Byrne, and halted on an island.

Little more than a willowed gravel bar, in the middle of the river. Sexsmith was giddy with fatigue. He insisted they make camp here.

This is quite picturesque. I'll call it little Albion. It's even shaped something like England, wouldn't you say, Viraj?

He strolled along the bank, prodding his stick in the stony earth.

You see, here is Southampton, the Solent. That rock out there is the Isle of Wight. It all works out.

There's no forage for the horses, Macpherson said. *On the far shore there's at least some goose-grass.*

Sexsmith would not listen. Macpherson led the horses across the shallow channel to the far bank, and stayed with them.

On the island, the other men built a fire with bleached driftwood. They roasted grouse and sang songs.

My boy's far away in the land that's called Canada
There would he go, though it left me lone and sad
O, 'twas gold he would gain to send home to
  his mother
Will he e'er come back to me, my little Irish lad

Sexsmith went for a stroll. He crossed a blue terrain of hummocks and hollows, climbed over Hadrian's Wall, to the upstream end of the island. The sky in the west was bright green over the black battlements of the mountains.

His senses were dulled by the long ride along the river flats, all except hearing. In the failing light he listened to the river rolling rocks in its bed. The rustle and click of willow shrubs in the evening wind.

The geese called, laughing in the dark.

wa hoh wa hoh wa hoh wa hoh wa hoh

He caught sight of them, a skein of five in a wavering line, letters of an unreadable word, shifting shape and position as they dwindled into distance.

31

At midnight Sexsmith blew out the starveling candle that lit his tent and stepped outside. He passed silently by Viraj, who was huddled by the remains of the watchfire, eyes closed.

Macpherson was standing on the far shore. When he saw Sexsmith he smiled easily, as though no distinctions of class and birth could cross the water between them.

In the west, above the black silhouette of the nearest ridge, the underbellies of low clouds glowed silver.

That light, said Sexsmith, raising his voice to be heard above the roar of water. *It was casting shadows on the wall of my tent.*

I've not seen such a thing before, Macpherson said. *The moon, shining on snow, I'd guess.*

Sexsmith lowered his voice to a whisper.

That's the place I've been seeking.

32

That night Sexsmith dreamed an old man in rusted armour, whose long white hair flowed out behind him in the wind from the west. He walked stiffly, held up more by the creaking metal carapace that enclosed him than by his own failing strength. Carrying his sacred trust, an object shrouded under a white cloth, across the plain and into the blue mountains.

Sexsmith walked beside him into the light from the setting sun. He looked down at himself and saw he was dressed in buckskin, with a buffalo robe draped over his shoulders.

Who are you? he asked the old man.

There were seven of us. I am the last one. We took an oath to follow the king into the west, and to keep the Grail hidden.

The old man stumbled at last and sank into the long grass. A gust of wind lifted the cloth and swept it away. The old man was holding a silver cup. At that moment the sun caught the lip of the cup and filled it with fire. The blazing light spilled over onto his armour, burnished it into white gold.

Sexsmith woke at dawn. His dream lingered with him, shining at the edges of his mind.

Viraj was at the campfire, brewing tea and heating water for the lord's morning shave. Sexsmith was surprised to see the young woman sitting beside him. The paint was gone from her face. Now she was only a thin girl warming herself by the fire. A cold, hungry mortal. The brothers stood nearby, talking with Macpherson, who had crossed back to the island with two pack ponies. Sexsmith scratched his stubbled neck. *Throat cutters.*

He sat down on the camp stool by the door of his tent, picked up one of his boots. The watchfire Viraj had tended outside his tent all night was cold ash. This was their fire, not his. Viraj brought him a cup of tea and he took it without speaking.

Elias, the younger brother, laughed. A quiet, pleasing laugh that made Sexsmith glance up. He liked Elias, his soft voice and unassuming manner.

Whatever Elias had said, it had even put a smile on Joseph's gaunt, scarred face. Sexsmith lowered his head and tugged on his boots. The word for a smile like that was *diabolical*.

Sexsmith looked up again just as Viraj handed the young woman a cup of tea.

33

When they reached dry ground, Sexsmith said,

The Stoneys were amused at something this morning.

Macpherson nodded.

Elias had a dream, sir. He thought it worth the telling.

Sexsmith called the brothers to him. He asked to hear the dream. Elias nodded.

I went with you to your city of London. There were plenty of buffalo there. I hunted them, with the Queen's sons. We chased buffalo over a jump. But when we went down to the bottom of the cliff, the animals had turned into books.

He grinned shyly at his brother and went on, in a near whisper.

The Queen's sons tried to read the books, but all the words were smashed in.

Sexsmith glanced at Joseph, whose gaunt face had withdrawn into grey immobility.

So tell me, Joseph. You are a wise fellow. Will you interpret your brother's dream?

34

The hunting party climbed a ridge that ran alongside a gently rising slope of dirty snow and ice.

Arcturus glacier, Sexsmith named it. *Bear watcher.*

Dark clouds were piled up over the peaks in the west. Macpherson expected snow at any time. He told Sexsmith that there would be no game at such an altitude.

The burn on the girl's palm, Sexsmith said. *If her map is accurate, we're just below it now. I want to know what's up there, what she's hiding from us.*

The young woman shook her head and spoke a few words to the Stoney brothers. Joseph turned to Sexsmith.

She's been there, he said. *In a dream. She says it's a spirit place. Not for the living.*

I'll find out for myself, Sexsmith said. *She's afraid of something. Something we'll discover if we go up there.*

The young woman would not look at him.

They got her from the Snakes, Sexsmith said to Viraj. *And we all know the serpent is the subtlest beast of the field.*

He sent everyone back down to the camp, told Macpherson to keep a close watch on the young woman. *She'll be ransom against my safe return.* He went on alone with the Stoney brothers.

35

It was late. Byrne and Sara sat facing each other in front of the stove. The flame of the candle on the shelf fluttered, drowning in its own wax. In the sepia gloom, Sara's skin resembled parchment.

—My father and the Company men stayed below in camp. While they waited the sun came out, and ice began to break off the wall of the glacier. The Company men gathered chunks of this broken ice that fell near them, to soothe the blisters on their hands and feet.

Sara knelt in front of the firebox, nudged the door open with a stick of stove wood and tossed it in. She stood up and turned towards Byrne.

—Athabasca came up to my father. She held out one of these broken pieces to him. He took it. It was exactly the size of a cricket ball, he told me, and looked like a blue-green diamond. He held it for a moment.

Sara cupped her hands around an invisible piece of ice.

—It burned.

Her hands moved apart.

—He dropped it. It was the first time he had been this close to ice. He had never touched it before.

36

Sexsmith and the brothers returned to camp the next evening. Macpherson was called into the lord's tent. A short time later he came back out to announce that the hunting trip was over. They would start back down in the morning.

The Company men grinned at one another. One of them brought out his fiddle, but Macpherson held up a hand in warning. Sexsmith was in a black mood. The sounds of celebration might give him cause to change his mind.

The fiddler set his fiddle down. He closed his eyes and began to tap his foot noiselessly on the earth. His fingers touched the strings of an invisible instrument. His body swayed to unheard music. The others stared at him and Macpherson shook his head and turned away. After another moment of hesitation the Company men slowly came together, choking back laughter, linking arms to dance a silent reel.

—What was it? Byrne asked. What turned Sexsmith back?

Sara shrugged.

—Snow, ice, she said. Maybe nothing more than that.

Byrne frowned, sat back in his chair.

—When I was in the crevasse. . . . He paused, rubbed his shoulder. What exactly did the girl mean . . . a spirit place?

—I don't know, Sara said. I was very young when she went away. I don't remember her.

—She was your mother.

—Yes.

On the return journey, Sexsmith came down with a chest cold. He stayed in his tent and refused to travel for several days. The hunting party camped on the river flats near the trading post.

The Stoney brothers told Viraj that their sister could be of help to the English lord.

Viraj went with this message to Sexsmith, who was bundled up in the buffalo robe he had taken back from Viraj, reading *The Tempest*. He did not care to be reminded of the world outside his canvas study.

I wish I could be transported back to England without leaving this tent. That would be pleasant indeed.

Viraj urged Sexsmith to let the young woman see him.

She may be able to help you, sir.

And then again she may be the death of me.

Viraj shook his head.

No.

Sexsmith swung the book upward and struck him on the side of the face.

You forget your place.

You are quite right, Viraj said.

He left the tent. He rode in a canoe with the Stoney brothers and the young woman, back to their fall camp on the far side of the river. When Sexsmith called for him he refused to come back.

Finally Sexsmith crossed over himself. In the Stoney camp, surrounded by willow racks of drying meat, they came to a gentlemanly agreement: Viraj was no longer in Sexsmith's service.

39

The next summer Athabasca took Viraj as her husband. They had a child the following year, and Viraj gave her the name Sarasvati. Her mother called her by another name, one from her own language.

In the fall, Joseph and Elias brought Viraj hunting with them, taught him to read the tracks of deer, moose, bear, wolf. And one other. A single print in the snow, invisible to Viraj until the brothers knelt beside it. Further on they found a camp and a pit of warm ashes in a narrow ravine. Joseph picked up a broken twig, its needles still bright green. It had been carried from somewhere else, from a tree that was unknown to Viraj, one that did not grow on this side of the mountains.

The Snake people, Joseph said.

When Viraj and the brothers returned to the Stoney camp, the Snake people came out of the forest after them like ghosts, four men, three women, a child. They had come into the valley from the west to trade furs and, though Athabasca did not remember them, she knew their stories.

One evening Athabasca gave Viraj the stone from around her neck. When the Snake people left that night, without a word, she went with them.

There was a storyteller in my village, Viraj said to Sara when she was much older, *who had one green eye. When I was a little boy I dared to ask him about it, and he told me his eye was green because his wife had left him. He said that long ago she wove a bolt of green cloth, the most beautiful that had ever been seen. He was very proud of what she had done, since it gave him great pres-*

tige in the village. Then one day his wife put on the green sari she had made from this cloth, walked out into the tall grass on the edge of the village, and disappeared. The storyteller searched for days and days, and sat by the tall grass, waiting, but she did not return. The storyteller leaned forward and pointed to his green eye. He said, Look closely and tell me if you see her.

Sarasvati grew up with her father. The people of the valley, the hunters and trappers and their children, found her name strange and difficult. They took her name, carried it around with them, stretched and scraped it like a strip of hide, wore it down into something more brief and familiar.

She was never called by the name her mother had given her, and in time it was forgotten. She became Sara.

40

Shouts, from the children outside, in the meadow.

Collie and Stutfield returned at last, alone. Thompson, Trask, and the wranglers had already started south for their headquarters in Banff. The two men strode into the cabin, sunburnt and wearily triumphant.

Collie had not found his mountain. He had stumbled upon a new world.

—The icefield, he said, eyes glittering in his wind-blasted face. I thought it would be an ordinary névé, feeding a single glacier. But it's huge, Ned. Stretches for miles. Greater than any *mer de glace* in the Alps. Breathtaking.

Stutfield nodded his agreement.

—We are probably the first human beings ever to see it. Definitely to have traversed it.

Byrne glanced at Sara. Her face was impassive. She knew he would say nothing, he read that much in her eyes. He was still afraid she had been lying. Weaving a smoke of fantasy around him that would shred away in the cold light of reason that entered the cabin with the two scientists.

—Think of it, Collie whispered. The last great remnant of the ice sheet that once covered this continent.

41

The next morning, Collie and Stutfield went to find Swift.

—I've never seen the icefield, Sara said as she waited with Byrne on the cabin steps. The great ice prairie, the Stoneys called it. A good place to stay away from. My father and I never went up there to see it for ourselves.

—Never? Byrne said. Living so close by all these years?

Sara shook her head and glanced up across the valley at the ice.

—In my father's country, he told me, the mountains are gods, or at least the palaces of gods. And, I think, for my mother's people as well. Spirit places. It was enough for us that we could see them from the valley.

42

Snow flurried through the morning air as Swift's cart, pulled by two lean horses, creaked up in front of the trading post.

Swift jumped down from the box of the cart with the agility of a cat. He wore a grey suit and necktie. His gaunt face was shadowed by a stetson, the brim of which he tipped toward Sara in a slow and deliberate mockery of politeness. His hawk eyes studied Byrne for a brief moment.

—Let's go, he said.

Byrne turned to Sara. He considered the few coins in his buttoned breast pocket, then decided against it.

—Thank you, he said.

She nodded and then said,

— Don't get lost, Swift.

Byrne was installed in a corner of the cart. He wrapped himself in a sleigh robe.

Swift flicked the reins and they jolted into motion. Collie and Stutfield rode ahead on two of the expedition ponies purchased from Trask. They were smiling, pleased with the morning air and with themselves, discoverers. Byrne glanced back at the cabin. Sara was gone from the doorway.

He sank back into the cushions and closed his eyes. The cart bumped and swayed along the track, lulling him. Bringing a rhythm, and a singsong voice, out of the past.

> *Doctor Foster went to Gloucester*
> *in a shower of rain*
> *he stepped in a puddle right up to his middle*
> *and never went there again.*

43

Sexsmith had to be satisfied with a black bear, a young male that Baptiste shot on the return trip. The Company men skinned the bear and cut it open. There were live ants in the stomach. One of the men took up the skin and danced with it around the fire, humming a Strauss waltz while the others laughed and clapped their hands.

Sexsmith examined the carcass, stripped to pink muscle. It looked like the naked body of a man. The hairless face grimaced at him in frozen hilarity.

❄

Byrne

*Not long after my return from the expedition I
began to keep a daily journal. It was intended to coin-
cide with what I considered to be the first flowering
of my mature life—my engagement to Martha, and
the securing of the post of assistant physician at Saint
Mary's Hospital. Looking through the pages now, in
1911, I see that for the first two years the journal kept
to that initial purpose, a concise chronicle of hopes and
achievements. But then, beginning in the winter of 1901,
it became a record of something very different.*

*Doubts about the meaning of the life I was pursu-
ing. Doubts about marriage and family life that most
men probably face if they give these matters serious
thought, but which in my case persisted and grew into
irrational fears. Attacks of panic in confined spaces or
unlit rooms. Waking in the middle of the night with
chest pains, a madly galloping heart, unable to draw
enough air into my lungs. Moments of unaccountable*

dread, and long hours of deep, harrowing sadness.

A delayed effect of the crevasse accident. That was my self-diagnosis. I wanted to believe it was merely a physiological problem, and I was determined to convince everyone else of this simple explanation for my increasingly erratic behaviour. I said nothing to Martha about the mental wrestling bouts that kept me awake throughout each night, the insidious voices that I knew well enough were coming from my own exhausted mind, not some demonic outside source, but that nevertheless counselled horrifying expedients to end this torment.

Writing alone seemed to keep my terror at bay, and so I recorded everything.

In less than a year I watched, incapable of any struggle on my own behalf, incapable even of anger or regret, as both my career and my engagement came to an end. Out of sheer financial necessity I began a private consulting practice. Patients were very few in number for some time, but this difficulty proved to be beneficial in that I thereby found the quiet and solitude that seemed to lessen the severity of my condition. Martha wrote to me and came to see me, but I closed myself off from her. I believe that she sensed there was something dreadfully wrong with me, that this behaviour was the cause rather than the result of my wish that our engagement be broken off. But as there was nothing she could do or say to make me confide in her, her attempts to breach my defenses eventually ceased. She called at my consulting

room one final time in the fall of 1903, to wish me well.
I have not spoken to her since.

Searching for an explanation at the time, I won-
dered whether this sudden fracturing of my world was
in some way connected to an illness I had gone through
as a child.

Lying like an invalid in Sara's cabin touched the
memory of that forgotten episode. I was nine years old.
My mother and my maternal grandmother, Nana, were
both still alive at that time. The seizures, as my father's
colleagues referred to them, began with a sensation of
dizziness and weakness in my limbs. I would have to lie
down, but I could not lie still. I shivered and my teeth
chattered, and after a few moments of this my body went
crazy. My eyeballs rolled back, my jaw twisted to one
side. My spine would bend and bend, backwards like a
bow, until I thought it would snap.

The procession of specialists who my father
brought in to examine me agreed on only one point: they
had no idea what was wrong with me. Epilepsy was
ruled out because I was conscious through the whole
ordeal. And each time it happened I got weaker. For a
while they thought I wouldn't live. No one said this to me,
but what with the candles and the visits from the priest
and the rosaries being thumbed night and day . . . well,
how could I not know? My mother even talked about
taking me to Lourdes, but my father wouldn't hear of it.
I remember his angry voice in the hall. I won't have

them waving incense over the boy and mumbling about unclean spirits. *He was convinced it was doing me no good to remain at home in this kind of atmosphere, and that I should be taken to the hospital where I would be kept under close observation by one of his colleagues. My mother would not consent to this, and to avoid the terrible arguments that began to erupt between her and my father, she took me with her to stay at my nana's house. And it was there that my mother and I prayed together without my father's intervention. We prayed and prayed, and then, one day, the attacks ceased. No gradual lessening of severity, they just vanished overnight. My mother called it a miracle.*

So it was that years later, after this childhood memory had been restored to me with every painful detail intact, I had to ask myself if the same malady that once seized hold of my limbs was now returning to life in my mind. As a boy I had apparently been witness to, or in some sense had embodied, a miracle. And as a young man I had again brushed close to something that defied rational understanding. I began to trace a thread in the fabric of my life that I had not cared to acknowledge before. A history growing in the shadows, obscured by the order I wished to see or impose on my experience. I believe that it was by taking hold of this thread, no matter how illusory it might have been, that I was able to find my way out of a labyrinth of madness rather than to continue to stumble towards its centre. From that moment I felt I had passed the crisis of the illness and began to grope my way slowly back to sanity.

Several years later I made the journey to Lourdes that I had not made as a boy, but I went as a tourist rather than a terminal case. The worst of the "hell" I had gone through was over, and I was only hoping this trip to France would provide some relief to my aching lungs, the last remnant of the misery that had all but consumed my life.

I was not expecting a miraculous cure, just an opportunity to breathe some less congested air, but when I first arrived in Paris I realized I would not get even that. For some reason I had imagined a city entirely unlike my own, one without London's unending procession of faces and bodies, a city without the smoke and the dirt and the soot.

On my second morning in Paris I went for a stroll along the Champs-Élysées. The day was hot, I had overdressed, and the crowd was swarming and darting around me like fish in an aquarium. I sat down on a bench. My sense of time and space was abruptly fogged. I had to think for a moment before I could remember the time of day, where I was and what I was doing there.

I closed my eyes. And then I was upside down again, hanging in the crevasse. The graceful, motionless figure there before me. All around us, silence and stillness. The meditation of ice and rock.

When I returned to London I went to the Society

headquarters in Savile Row, to see Professor Collie. He
and Stutfield had been back to the Rockies several times
since the first expedition. They'd rediscovered Mount
Brown, found it to be a relatively minor peak, and had
then named and climbed some of the giants that ring
the icefield: Arcturus, Diadem, The Brothers, Parnassus.

We sat together in the Society tea room. Two
confirmed bachelors. He and his mentor in chemistry,
William Ramsay, had recently isolated a new element,
neon. He talked about it with his customary vigour, how
the excitation of the gas molecules produces a rather
pleasing illumination, one that might have some
interesting uses for commercial lighting.

I brought up the subject of his further icefield
explorations, but I knew I was avoiding the very thing
I had hoped to discuss: what I had seen in the crevasse.
I had never said a word about my experience to anyone,
not even to Martha. And now, in this cathedral of skepti-
cism and science, I found myself unwilling to speak of
it. In fact I panicked for a moment when the thought
occurred to me that I had not only imagined the figure
in the crevasse, but that the entire expedition was only
a fantasy of mine, a hallucination, and were I to mention
anything about my part in it, Collie would stare at me,
knit his brows, and say something like I'm afraid I don't
know what you're talking about, Byrne. You weren't
on that expedition. As I recall, we only discussed it
briefly at Kew, and you declined the invitation. Now

perhaps you'd better let me accompany you to the hospital. . . .

    I recognized this irrational fear as a faint echo of what I suffered during the many sleepless nights spent at my desk, furiously writing. Trying to convince myself, by retracing the events of my life in meticulous detail, that I was not going insane, and how, in reading what I had written about my own life, a similar cold terror had washed over me that none of it had really happened. That it was someone else's life, or a baseless fabrication of my crumbling mind. At that time the terror of this thought was magnified a thousandfold by fatigue and my already distraught condition. But now, sitting in a comfortable leather armchair, in the oak-panelled tea room with its spears and ritual masks hanging innocuously from the walls, I was able to remain at least outwardly calm. The fear passed as quickly as it had come, but I knew then that the chance to speak my mind had passed.

    I could see that Collie guessed there was some unspoken purpose behind all my questions, and after a while we both lapsed into silence.

    At the far end of the room sat an explorer recently returned from Asia, surrounded by an eager audience. His stentorian voice reached to where we sat and we were forced to listen to his rather self-glorifying monologue. I remember him saying A godawful place, the Gobi. And yet lovely. I quite liked it. It resembled my mind. ✤

MORAINE

ROCK DEBRIS DEPOSITED BY THE RECEDING ICE:

A CHAOTIC JUMBLE OF FRAGMENTS, FROM WHICH

HISTORY MUST BE RECONSTRUCTED.

1

An item clipped by Byrne from the *London Times* (1907):

> *Jasper Forest Park, a national game preserve, has been established by the Dominion government, along the western boundary of the newly-created Province of Alberta.*
>
> *Within the boundaries of this new preserve, hunting, trapping, and unauthorized settlement are prohibited.*

A railway is now proposed for this region, to rival the Canadian Pacific line to the south. Anton Sibelius, one of the major financiers of the venture, has said: "The Jasper game and forest preserve, similar to that created at Banff, will ensure the virginal beauty of this remote wilderness is not defiled, that it can be enjoyed forever by travellers, mountain climbers, and seekers after solitude."

2

—That woman, Trask says, blowing out a cloud of smoke. Now there's a tale.

Four years after pasting the clipping from the *Times* into his notebook, Byrne is in Jasper Forest Park, in a garden under glass, telling the story of the expedition.

He is a guest at Frank Trask's chalet, invited to afternoon tea in the glasshouse. He came late, not knowing what to expect, and his first surprise was the young woman, Elspeth Fletcher, who greeted him in the lobby. She was quite young, Scottish by her accent, and quietly self-assured. She escorted him to the glasshouse, introduced him to everyone there, then returned with a tray of refreshments, and stayed to listen while he told his story.

He says nothing to Trask's assembled guests about what he saw in the crevasse. When he comes to the place where he must speak of Sara, he hesitates.

—Of course I don't remember how we got to her cabin. I've merely borrowed Frank's version of the events.

Trask folds his arms across his chest.

—You're telling it fairly, doctor. Although I'd put more emphasis on the bravery of the young guide who saved your skin.

Clouds of steam rise from the bubbling mineral fountain in the glasshouse. Water drips from the broad, sagging leaves of hothouse plants. Down the glass panes, droplets of condensation slide, so that the windows seem to be melting in the heat.

While Trask takes over the conversation, Byrne settles back in his chair. Through the fogged windows he can make out the jagged silhouettes of spruce trees rocking slightly in the wind. He would like to step outside into the cool mountain evening.

He is the doctor for the mountain section of the Grand Trunk Pacific, where the line is being doubled in expectation of increased overland traffic. In the fall he will return to London and another doctor will take over his duties.

The field hospital where he lives and works is a giant canvas tent with a red cross painted on its roof, set up and dismantled to keep pace with the advancing construction. His spartan living quarters are behind a screened enclosure in a corner of the hospital.

There are many accidents on the line. The men work themselves into exhaustion trying to battle unexpected obstacles, like the creeping sand dunes along the river flats that bury the same section of track every few days. Dysentery and other ailments are rife in the crowded, unsanitary camps. Byrne is kept busy.

When he makes his infrequent visits to the chalet or the town, he finds himself surrounded with the comforts of the twentieth century. As a special guest of Trask, he has been lodged in a cozy chalet room with a fireplace and running water. There are oystershell electric lamps and palm trees in the lobby. If he wanted to, he could sit at an oak desk in the lounge, under a delicate bowl of light, and write letters home to England.

3

—I'd like to hear more, Father Buckler says, about what it was like in the crevasse.

—Cold, says Byrne. Everyone laughs. Byrne hesitates, searching for words. Frank Trask leans forward in his chair, pounces on the unwanted silence.

—That's right. Cold. But you didn't have to be at the bottom of a crevasse to feel it. The whole valley was inhospitable.

The 1898 expedition was Trask's first as a head guide.

They had started from Banff in search of Collie's prize, and he had found his own. A wild valley waiting for a resourceful young man to see its potential.

Now he is part-owner of the chalet and its marvelous glasshouse, half a day's journey by train from the growing town of Jasper. It was he who convinced the railway magnates to build a spur line from the wide Athabasca valley into this more remote and colder region of the mountains.

He has a responsibility to ensure that conversation travels a smooth path, and so he leads it, like a string of pack ponies, out of deadfall and other difficulties.

—Cold and desolate. I came west from Bruce County, Ontario, at the age of sixteen, my head stuffed with foolish notions. There wasn't much in Banff, and less than nothing here. Whatever I had, I had to make for myself. And now look at the place. I've got a theory. You can measure the progress a frontier settlement makes by counting how many fewer dogs there are roaming the streets every year.

He drops back heavily into the comfort of his velvet-backed chair, waves his cigarette with a flourish.

—All this in a decade. I'm sure Doctor Byrne agrees it's a change for the better.

Byrne smiles and sips from his tea cup.

Trask takes note of the admiring glances directed at the doctor. A romantic figure to those who keep to the immaculate lawns that girdle the chalet and go no further. Elspeth certainly seems to like him. Reserved, cultured, gentlemanly, and yet he was trapped down in that crevasse, during a dangerous expedition. It could, Trask muses, be turned into a profitable curiosity. The man who was trapped in the jaws of icy death. The *icy* jaws of death might be better. Trask wonders if he could persuade Byrne to lead guided walking tours up to the glacier. *It might work. If he wasn't such a stiff-necked bastard.*

4

—There must be a fantastic view of the icefield from the summit of Arcturus.

Byrne glances up at the sound of the voice. Freya Becker, the travel writer.

—I'm tackling it this summer, she says. What about a teahouse up there, Mr Trask?

Byrne studies her. The notorious Miss Becker. Pilloried by the Canadian papers for her one-woman attack on the male bastion of mountaineering. He had heard of her before she came to Jasper, and this is not the woman he had imagined. Not this slender, sunburned girl who stirs restlessly in her chair.

—A hot drink at the summit would fetch any price you'd dare charge.

—It's a thought, Trask says without looking at her. The more civilized we can make things, the better.

Next to Freya Becker sits Hal Rawson, the young poet working for Trask as a trail guide. He has not said a word yet this afternoon. When Byrne catches his eye he looks away.

5

—It was from Arcturus that Collie first saw the icefield, Byrne says. And according to him, yes, the view was magnificent.

Byrne is aware he has been invited here as a kind of special treat for the people who make up Jasper's frontier society. He is the Englishman. Trask expects him to display certain qualities thought to be lacking this far west in the Dominion: nobility of sentiment, decorum, a cool reserve lightened by gleams of urbane wit. He has had much practice in playing the role and this afternoon it comes easily to him.

He is also aware of Elspeth Fletcher, the hostess. The fact that their eyes happen to meet whenever he glances her way.

This garden under glass is her creation.

A rock pool with a fountain bubbles in the centre of the glasshouse. The water is pumped in from the hot spring.

Humid air fills the glasshouse like a rippling green liquid. Byrne watches the other men pulling at their collars, and he wonders how Elspeth can remain so unruffled, so cool and intact in this heat.

This is the first time Byrne has seen the chalet's glasshouse. He remembers the tiny native flowers he collected on the expedition, the precariousness of their existence. Here in this garden, sealed off from the glacial winds, are giant, unabashed blossoms from Europe, India, the Pacific islands. *Camellia fictilia* growing next to hyacinth. The effort, the likely cost of such a display, astounds him.

—This region has had a lot of names, Trask says, but Jasper is the one that stuck.

He leans forward, flicks cigarette ash on the glasshouse's stone floor, then darts a worried glance in Elspeth's direction. He grins, gives her a stage wink.

—The old Métis settlement called Jasper was near here. During the fur trade it was called Snow House, or Arcturus House, but some of the natives called it Jasper. Then when Yellowhead Pass was chosen as the rail route over the Divide, the town had to be located further down in the Athabasca valley. It's wider there, of course, less of a grade for the railroad, and not so beastly cold. Jasper wasn't the first choice for a name, though. We called the place Fitzhugh for a while, in honour of one of the railroad moguls. When it was still just a tent city.

—Jasper, Elspeth says. I've wondered about that. Where the name came from.

Trask shrugs.

—That's what the traders and Indians called it. As to why, I couldn't say. Sara, the woman who minded Doctor Byrne for us, she was here before Christ —pardon me, Father—so she might know. But I wouldn't take it as gospel.

—Why not? Freya Becker says.

—Well, Miss Becker, Trask says slowly, you should ask the doctor that question.

—All right, I will. Doctor Byrne?

Byrne looks up, startled, at their wondering faces.

—Excuse me. I'm sorry. I was admiring the flowers.

Trask grunts.

—Still mourning your lost treasures, I suppose. That's the thanks I get.

—I always kept the seeds and bulbs with me, but I didn't want you to know that at the time. No offense, but your pack ponies were rather good at scraping their cargo off against trees. I was hoping to get some British Columbian specimens when we crossed the Divide.

—You were the expedition botanist, Father Buckler says, as well as the doctor?

—Not officially. It's just that camp life turned out have its monotonous side.

—Purgatory, it's been called, Trask says.

—Yes. I hadn't expected that. For the first few days I was living the romance of camp life. And then at night I started dreaming about my featherbed at home. After a while the only topic of conversation around the fire was our favourite restaurants. Collecting the flowers kept my mind busy.

Elspeth rises and refills his tea cup.

—I believe Miss Becker wanted to hear more about Sara.

Byrne smiles. He will tell them about Sara. He will not tell them everything.

7

The guests drink their tea, help themselves to cucumber and orange slice sandwiches. Trask tells mountain legends and bear stories. The party lingers into the evening.

Byrne takes a sip from his cup. The tea has gone cold.

Elspeth knows the right moment. She rises and asks her guests to follow her down the stone path to the back gate. They stroll through a tunnel of thick foliage.

Elspeth unlocks the narrow wooden door and swings it open. Gelid air streams into the glasshouse. Like rubbing alcohol it lifts away the film of sweat from Byrne's skin.

—Now this is wonderful, Freya Becker says. She stretches out her arms. Yes.

The glasshouse fills with a milky, luminescent fog, and the guests watch one another grow pale and fade. Cool droplets condense like a cold sweat on their faces and arms. Feathery snowflakes appear above them, drifting down on their heads, on the leaves of the tropical flowers.

When they have all gathered outside, Elspeth quickly shuts the door behind them.

—The flowers don't like it as much as we do.

The conversation is revived by the cool air, the keen scent of pine and spruce. While they stand at the back gate and talk, twilight seems to bring the mountains closer around them. Patches of snow gleam like phosphors against the dark rock.

Hal Rawson steps out the furthest into the shadows. He turns and regards the others through the arabesques of his cigarette smoke, his expression unreadable.

Trask frowns at him, clears his throat.

—Now, Doctor, I understand you're also back in Jasper to study glaciers.

—That's right.

Trask shakes his head.

—You're a persistent sort, Byrne, I'll grant you that. But I'm afraid if you get swallowed up I won't be around this time to come to your rescue. So don't do anything foolish, please.

Rawson's sudden voice out of the dark:

—The glaciers creep like snakes that watch their prey.

The guests glance at one another. Another awkward silence falls. Elspeth opens her mouth to speak, then purses her lips.

—Shelley, I believe, Byrne says, coming to someone's rescue, Rawson's or Miss Fletcher's. Or both.

—From his poem *Mont Blanc*. It's curious: in 1816 Shelley apparently understood that glaciers once covered most of Europe. In that poem he imagines an ice age, an idea that scientists scoffed at for another thirty years.

Rawson flicks his cigarette away. There is evidently nothing more to be said. Elspeth turns and smiles at Byrne.

—It's fascinating when you think about it. The fact that a glacier moves, I mean, but so slowly that you can't see it.

Byrne raises his cup of cold tea, pours a little out into the saucer.

—Think of this saucer filling to its rim and then spilling over. A glacier is an overflow from a great saucer of rock that has filled with ice over the millennia. It pours out, one could say, wherever there is a gap between the encircling peaks.

He tips the saucer and a few drops spill onto the paving stones with an unmistakable dribbling sound. Trask coughs out a cloud of cigar smoke and Freya laughs. Byrne goes on in a chastened tone,

—Eleven thousand years ago, it's estimated, the ice covered this entire valley.

Elspeth watches Byrne as he speaks. He is ten years her senior and looks much older, weatherworn. His manner is distant, reserved. She feels a momentary desire to touch his face, imagining it would be as cool and impervious as marble.

He has returned to the mountains after more than a decade. To the place where he nearly lost his life. She wants to know why.

8

The next morning Byrne leaves the chalet on a chestnut mare from Trask's stable and rides along the creek. He follows the windings of a sinuous esker to the site of the old settlement, although he knows he will find it deserted.

—The settlers were kicked out four years ago, Trask told Byrne as he helped him saddle up. When the national park was created. Well, most of them got compensation or deeds to land further north. So it wasn't totally ruthless, you see. They weren't driven off with guns.

Only those who had sanctioned business within the boundaries, guides and trailblazers like Trask, were allowed to remain.

—Swift's still here, Trask said. Nobody was going to order him off his land. And prime real estate it is. I only wish I'd seen it first.

9

At the old settlement Byrne realizes how much the Arcturus glacier has receded, the advance made by trees, grasses, flowers, into the barren valley. What is strange, what can only be a trick of memory, is that the cabins themselves are much farther from the river bank than he remembers, tucked in a stand of dark trees, as if they too have been receding with the ice.

The trading post is gone. He is sure of that. None of the remaining log ruins show traces of the trellised portico, the narrow windows, that he remembers. He dismounts, ground-ties the mare and enters one of the cabins that has no door. Inside it is bare, the dark logs streaked with light from the gaps in the sagging roof. A willow is growing in through the window.

In the silence he speaks aloud the words he imagined he would say to her.

—Do you have any more stories to tell?

Byrne follows the course of Arcturus Creek to the till plain. Here he dismounts again and leads the horse. This flat stretch of sand, gravel, and braided streams has lengthened in the years since he was last here. Dividing it are the moraines, curving outerworks of recessional rubble, resembling the concentric walls of an ancient Celtic fortress. Each time he struggles to the top of a moraine, Byrne finds that the glacier is still farther away than he thought it would be.

Twelve years before, when the expedition established its base camp here, the glacier terminus was a high wall of cracked pinnacles surrounding a wide cave entrance. He fancied it resembled a giant marble foot, all that remained of some forgotten colossus. Now there is only a rounded slope buried at its end in a mound of wet mud and rock, the debris laid bare by recession.

Perhaps this is a landscape better suited to a rational new century.

In the evening he returns to the old settlement and sets up camp near the cabin he entered before.

Night falls swiftly and the mare, tethered to a krummholz stand, lifts the black silhouette of her head against the moonlit clouds.

Byrne leaves the dying fire and crawls inside the cabin.

10

My Dear Loved Ones:

I'm sure you've been wondering at the long delay since I last wrote, and now that the mail service has been restored, I can tell you the reason. We've just had a flood.

Apparently a dam of loose ice built up downstream, and with the spring melt already underway, there was a lot of water coming down from the glaciers. I woke up on the first morning of the flood to see ducks paddling down a river that had once been the road past the chalet. I also heard that a black bear, driven away from its feeding grounds by the rising water, took refuge on the roof of Mr. Trask's house. For the next three days our little corner of the world could have been described in one word: slush.

When the dam burst, slabs of blue ice tumbled down the swollen river, surfacing and diving like sapphire dolphins. Trees were sheared off the crumbling banks. Further down the valley in Jasper, the ground buckled and doors no longer closed. Headstones in the cemetery sank into the spongy earth. The ends of coffins rose up like the prows of sinking ships.

The Anglican church, a hopeful wooden structure, collapsed during the first night of the flood. In the morning the townspeople found a saint standing in the river, grounded upright on a gravel bar. The wooden statue wobbled unsteadily in the rushing current, birds perched on one of its outstretched, nut-brown arms.

Two days ago it was snowing, and yesterday I was helping with the cleanup and got a bit of a sunburn. It feels wonderful to be outside a lot more though, even with this crazy weather.

I must close now. Morning comes very early, and I have a full day ahead. A world of love. From your loving daughter,

Elspeth

11

The morning after the glasshouse party she is in the chalet's front parlour, sipping hot Earl Grey tea from an eggshell china cup.

From her window, she can just make out a climbing team struggling up the glacier against blowing snow. Five tiny figures huddled together, crawling slowly forward up the slope. The alpinists from Zermatt.

Elspeth blows on the surface of the steaming tea, sips from it, raises her head and listens.

Above the sound of the wind, she hears the distant crack and crumple of an avalanche. The thin glass in the windowframe rattles. She glances out. It takes her a moment to find the source, a slender white plume flowing down a dark seam of Mount Arcturus. The avalanche is high on the mountain and the alpinists are in no danger, but they stand motionless, watching as the cascade of snow and ice bursts over a rock ledge.

So graceful and delicate from this distance, as if unconnected to the thunder echoing across the valley. At the glasshouse party Byrne had told her there could be chunks of ice the size of train cars falling in those powdery veils.

Elspeth takes another sip of tea, pleased with the bitterness of lemon.

12

In 1910 she came to Jasper from Inverness, having managed a tea and pastry shop there. A Canadian aunt of hers had met Trask while on a railway excursion through the Rockies. In the dining car Trask went on about his new "glacier" chalet, the difficulty of finding good staff. The aunt mentioned her niece. A bright young woman. Diligent. Level-headed and absolutely trustworthy.

Trask wrote Elspeth a letter in which he asked her such questions as *Do you smoke?* and *How tall are you?* and *What colour is your hair?*

Elspeth was twenty-three years old. She was unmarried. This was an adventure.

She answered everything truthfully except the question about smoking. And instead of telling him her hair was red, which might mark her as hot-tempered, she wrote *auburn.*

She stepped off the train that first day to be met by one of Trask's men. He said hardly a word, seemed unwilling to look at her. She understood later he was bearing the weight of his good fortune, being the one chosen to meet *the young lady.*

The older woman she had shared a compartment with, who was going on to Victoria, came out during the brief stop to take her picture.

—Let's get you and the young gentleman here, and the train, together.

Elspeth and the guide were obliged to step off the platform. Watching the woman with the camera, Elspeth stood in a patch of spring snow. Instantly the felt travel slippers she had been wearing on the train were soaked through. She smiled for the photograph, her feet throbbing with cold.

13

The day's tasks are finished, but her mind is still a hawk, holding her limp body upright in its talons. She is little more than thought. As bodiless as light.

At this time of night she goes to the hot spring pool to be alone, to steam away this nervous residue of energy leftover from the work day. But tonight the team of alpinists from Switzerland is still there. They returned late from the glacier, shivering, wet, and hungry.

The alpinists in the pool are celebrating, splashing, howling back at the coyotes calling from the black hillside above the chalet. In from the cold and dark, they are giddy with joy at the comforts of civilization. Hot running water, wine and cheese, the anticipation of a warm feather bed.

Elspeth steps out onto the promenade. She sees a tiny glimmer of light in the darkness. A lantern. Someone is still out there, coming along the trail from the glacier. The first person she thinks of is Hal Rawson.

Elspeth makes her way down the steps of the promenade and along the gravel path, lined with whitewashed stones, that leads toward the creek. She lights a cigarette. This is the only place, and time, that she has the privacy to smoke.

She walks along the path, to the wooden bridge over the creek. On the far side of the bridge, the broad, stone-lined path gives way to a rough dirt trail that snakes into the forest. The soft earth there, at the end of the paved path, holds the imprint of many passages. The delicate impression of a woman's fashionable shoe. A grizzly paw print.

Elspeth walks to the middle of the bridge and leans against the rail, smoking, looking down into the black water. Some nights she meets other people on the bridge, often couples who have found this to be a likely setting for romance.

This is a cold night, and the bridge is deserted. Elspeth finishes her cigarette and flicks it over the railing. Sometimes she can hear, above the roar of water, the brief hiss as the spark is extinguished.

The light she saw on the promenade is now much closer. It bobs and flickers through the trees at the head of the path. She hears the *chock* of a horse's hoof on stone. Then a man appears with a lantern raised over his head. At first she can see only a hand, the silhouette of a hat, and behind it, the dark bulk of the horse being led. The hand lowers the lantern, and Byrne's face appears. He looks shocked to see her.

14

The next morning Elspeth finds an envelope from Byrne left for her at the front desk of the chalet. She tears it open. Inside, a small filing card.

Miss Fletcher:
I hoped to see you today, but I've been called to an
accident down the line.

Ned Byrne

She turns the page over. Nothing else.
I hoped to see you today.

15

The morning he left the note for Elspeth, Byrne was taken on a handcar to the construction site. There had been an accidental dynamite blast. A man, the fore-man told him, had been nailed to the rock cut by a flying spike.

The injured man stood upright, as if resting against the rock face, the rest of the crewmen gath-ered in a half-circle around him. He whispered to himself, his right arm held outstretched, the fingers of his pinioned hand opening and closing around the spike. Examining him, Byrne found he had been struck in the abdomen as well, probably by a frag-ment of rock.

When Byrne probed the stomach wound, the man opened his eyes. He screamed once, a brief, hoarse cry of agony, and fainted.

There was no morphine. Byrne administered bromide of potassium as a sedative. He decided it would be best to wait for the end and then cut him down.

Towards evening the man woke up again. One of the crewmen cut a makeshift crucifix out of blue paper. He held it up to the injured man, who fixed his eyes on it, his lips moving noiselessly.

The vigil beside the dying man lasted into the night. The man who had held up the blue paper cross stayed with Byrne after the others drifted away. He stroked the injured man's head and answered him softly when he spoke out in fitful moments of consciousness. The speech of the two men lapsed in and out of Italian, a language Byrne did not know, although he caught a few familiar words. *Maria. Acqua. Madre.* Finally he realized the men were brothers.

At dawn, Byrne woke to the sound of a giant heartbeat. He lifted his head from the roll of canvas he had been dozing fitfully against. The section crew was back at work, hammering down the rails.

The man's brother stood over him. He held out his hand and helped Byrne to his feet. Byrne took the magnifying lens from his satchel and held it to the man's mouth. There was no condensation.

The crewmen stopped work and came over when they saw Byrne. He left the body in their care and walked stiffly alongside the track to the cluster of tents beside the lake. The water glittered with fragments of sun. Cloud shadows slid across the white dunes. A glorious morning.

Byrne found coffee and a leftover bread roll in the empty mess tent. He ate quickly and then wrote out his report. Later the section foreman came in, sat down beside Byrne, and began to talk.

He had once helped build a railroad into the gold fields of Colombia. There, the trains often came under attack by bandits. The gold-carrying cars had to be sheathed in steel and guarded by armed men. But then it often happened that the overloaded trains, and the rails themselves, were swallowed up in the swamps.

—Here, the foreman said, there's nothing. No gold in the rocks, in the rivers. Nothing but grass and wind. Why put in a railroad?

From outside, the shriek of a hawk. The two men looked past the tent flap snapping in the wind, at the bright wedge of sunlit dunes.

16

The foreman's tale, which Byrne set down in his notebook as he rode the handcar back to town:

It happened years before, on the Canadian Pacific

railhead far to the south, in the Kicking Horse Pass.

To the foreman's crew, the Swan glacier resembled a woman in flowing skirts. They nicknamed her Anastasia, joked about the spunk that would be needed to thaw her icy disdain. One night the foreman saw this ice maiden at the window of his hut. Like moonlight she entered his sleeping compartment. She glided down to where he lay, whispering softly, and kissed him with frozen lips.

In the morning, the rail crew discovered that two hundred metres of track near the bunkhouse were buried under the snout of the surging Swan glacier.

They found the foreman lying on the floor of his cabin, without blankets, shivering. He came down with pneumonia and spent a week in bed, feverish and incoherent.

—I was babbling of green fields, the foreman said. And the whore of Babylon, too, no doubt.

The rail workers kept bonfires burning for two weeks, to speed up the melting of the glacier. At last the buried stretch of line was exposed. They shovelled away heaps of slush and found a section of track torn up from its gravel bed, the two steel rails twisted around each other like twining snakes.

Two days later Byrne returns from the construction site. He and Elspeth make an excursion to the till plain. Clouds shroud the peaks and a cold mist descends around them. Byrne shrugs.

—I'm sorry I can't predict the weather.

—I grew up with this, she says. It's the Scot way of basking in the sun.

—In the glasshouse you were wondering about the origin of the town's name. That's what I wanted to see you about the other day, before I was called out to the accident.

—Yes?

—Warden Langford traces the name to an early fur trader named Jasper Hawes. But I think it was possibly derived from the French phrase *j'espère*: I hope.

—Why is that?

—An early surveyor spelled it *Jespare* in his published journal. What local meaning this phrase has I don't know. But on one old map the region is labeled *Despair*, which might be a further corruption of the original French phrase.

—Well, the next time I'm asked about the name, I'll have an answer.

A spruce tree appears ahead of them. Its branches emerge out of the haze into sudden sharp clarity. A tree so green in the shrouded landscape it seems to be the only living thing in a world of ghosts.

Taking shelter under the branches of the tree, they share coffee from Elspeth's vacuum flask. Byrne holds his tin cup in both hands, near his mouth. It has been a long time since he has been alone with a woman. And she is almost a stranger. When Elspeth is not looking he studies her bare, slender neck, her hair neatly gathered under her straw hat, the small pale wrinkle beside her mouth when she smiles, perhaps a scar from a childhood injury.

—Frank told me you were the last person he expected to see in Jasper again.

—That's what I thought, too.

18

Bundled up in Swift's cart as the Collie expedition headed for Edmonton, he told himself he would never return.

When the sooty arches of the Victoria railway terminus appeared out of a grey London drizzle, he was certain of that. He was home.

There was no one at the station to greet him, as he had planned. He had written to his father, and to Martha, while still in hospital in Edmonton, but had been deliberately vague about when he would be arriving. This way he would be free, at least for a while, from questions and concerns about his health. He felt there was an invisible boundary he had to pass through, alone and in silence, in order to reenter the world he had left only five months before.

The first thing he did upon entering his flat was to light a fire in the grate, with the remnants left in the coal scuttle. He stood by the door in his overcoat, waiting for warmth to make the room his own again.

19

He tells Elspeth of his discovery of the ice-cored moraine running through the chalet grounds.

—It was about a week after I first arrived. Frank took me out here to show off his creation, and I saw right away that there would be a problem.

He said nothing at first to Trask, whose one complaint about the site was that the well buckets often came up filled with slush.

For some time he was busy studying a detailed relief map. At last he wrote a letter to the railway company.

An ancient glacial moraine runs under part of the railroad grade, and alongside the chalet grounds. This moraine still has a core of glacial ice that was buried by rock and never melted. I recommend that you find another location for your proposed hot spring pool, otherwise you may find the present site prone to destabilization.

When Trask heard about the doctor's recommendation, he was furious.

—It's one hell of a tall tale, Byrne.

—It's true.

Trask leaned over the chalet railing and spat.

—As true as that woman's stories. Yeah, I heard them too: 'My father was a maharajah and my mother was a snake woman.' Christ.

Byrne stared at Trask.

—That's right, doctor, I'm telling you it was all horse manure. Here's my version: she was a fatherless brat hanging around the trading post, and some fool made the mistake of teaching her how to read. *Arabian Nights* and *Tales of King Arthur,* that's where she got her life story.

The railway company sent out their own geologists, who verified Byrne's findings. The railroad had to be diverted slightly for several hundred feet, and the hot spring pool was built higher up on the hill behind the chalet. Trask met the doctor in town one day and whispered,

—No more icy surprises, please.

20

While they sit together under the spruce tree, the mist rises and dissipates. In the widening sky, wraiths of rain clouds drift. Sunshine lights up the far slopes of the valley. Elspeth and Byrne are still within the cool shadow of the mountain wall.

—One thing you can depend on here, Byrne says, is the changeable weather.

A raven flaps overhead, croaks once as it climbs into the sky. It weaves slowly from side to side, loops around once as its wings ride the wind currents. Just before the dark shape dwindles in the distance to invisibility, they see it veer to the left, away from the bright, forested side of the valley. The raven comes into sharp black focus against the white gleam of snow, as it glides down into a glacial cirque.

—Why would it choose the dead side? Elspeth says.

—It's a scavenger, Byrne says. An opportunist. Chance meals always show up more clearly in the snow. And more often, too, I would imagine.

—That's another tidbit I can pass on to the guests.

—It sounds like you get a lot of strange questions.

—Yes, but I don't mind. I like talking to people. Most people. It's the ones who won't deign to say a word to me that make my blood boil.

She smiles.

—Once or twice I've come close to ruining things for myself. There was one old fellow, he put so much effort into being oblivious to my existence. He would tap his saucer with a spoon, and carry on this lofty conversation with his wife while I poured the tea. When I dared ask him a question he'd stare past me and his wife would answer for him. It drove me mad, but after a while I thought it was funny. If I had suddenly dropped to the floor in a dead faint, I'm sure he would've stepped right over me without a word and gone on his way. I almost tried it, just to see what he'd do.

—Then I hope for your sake my father doesn't visit. That sounds something like him, although in his case it's not deliberate. He's too busy thinking about his work to notice the rest of the human race. The man is nearly seventy and he's just started working on another textbook. *The Principles of Obstetrics.*

—He's a doctor, too.

—Yes, although now he mostly lectures and writes. Kate, his wife, told me he ate and slept in his study for two weeks while he was finishing the last book.

—She must be a patient soul.

—She is. With me, too, in those first years. I'm afraid I made things difficult for her then. But she never said a word about it. And now when I write home, she's the one I write to, if I want a reply. When I write to my father the letters end up in a stack on the floor.

—What do they think of your coming back to Jasper to work?

—I never asked.

Byrne glances up into the sunlight.

—We'd better start back while this good weather holds.

21

Byrne hires one of Trask's guides to help him haul supplies to Arcturus glacier. Hal Rawson, who had startled Trask's guests with his quote from Shelley.

Byrne and Rawson ride out to the glacier, bringing along a pack pony loaded with the doctor's gear. Rawson sets up camp, cooks, and cares for the horses, while Byrne spends the day on the ice.

In the evening Byrne returns to camp, exhausted, sunburnt, taciturn. He sits under the hanging lantern, absorbed in his sketches and field notes.

—Would you like something to eat, doctor?

Byrne looks up in surprise at Hal, who is holding out to him a plate of mutton stew. He had forgotten he is not alone.

—This seems pretty earthy work for a man of letters, Byrne says.

—Or for a man of medicine, Rawson says, and

blushes. He swallows a mouthful of food, makes a grimace.

—Pretty earthy stew, as well. My apologies.

They share a laugh.

—No, Rawson says, this place wasn't quite what I imagined it would be.

22

Hal Rawson first disembarked at the Jasper station on a chilly May evening. He was advised by telegram to wait for the carriage from the chalet.

A few tourists milled about, muffled in overcoats, stamping their feet in front of the stove. Voices were low and weak. A hall of strangers. Rawson found a vacant place on a bench and from his valise took a shiny new leatherbound book. Collie and Stutfield's *Climbs and Explorations*. His father's parting gift.

A little boy in a navy jacket ran across the room clutching a Noah's ark. He collided with Rawson's legs.

An explosion of toy animals. Rawson caught one tiny figurine as it fell: a white bird. He handed it to the boy who was already kneeling, gathering his scattered menagerie. A young woman in a huge fur coat smiled at Rawson as she led the boy back to his seat, her gaze charged with some emotion that drove him to glance down quickly at his book.

Carriages arrived and carried the tourists away to fireplaces and warm beds. The sound of harness bells, hooves on packed snow, growing distant. Soon there were only two people left sitting in the station hall. Rawson and an old man across from him. The stationmaster, chained to his pocketwatch, eyed them with suspicion.

From an inner room the telegraph clicked at a breathless pace. Drowsily, Rawson wondered whether the receiver could sense the emotion of the sender in those disembodied dots and dashes.

The old man said a few words in a language Rawson did not understand. Smiling, he held up a bottle. Greek lettering. Retsina. Rawson declined with a shake of his head. The old man made a face, a grotesque parody of sorrow. He took a drink and wiped his mouth on his sleeve.

The stationmaster cleared his throat, nodded sternly toward the entrance. The old man sighed, slipped the bottle into a coat pocket and stood up. He smiled at Rawson, held his hands up by his ears and fluttered them like wings as he shuffled out the door.

23

The next morning Rawson met his new employer, Frank Trask, at the chalet office. On the wall hung a framed photograph Rawson recalled having seen before, in a book on the opium war in China. A portrait of three convicted smugglers, decapitated moments before the image was captured. Their executioner standing to one side, uninterested in the result of his work, examining his blade. Three heads, with contorted faces like masks representing Tragedy, lined up in the grass before the bodies. And a boldface caption: **Don't Lose Your Head.**

Trask no longer personally supervised the pack trains. But this day he appeared in his old boots, dungarees, and buckskin jacket to welcome the new man. He strode across the yard, Rawson following cautiously, sidestepping mounds and puddles.

—I'll show you around the outfit—bunkhouse, stables, corral. Oh, and of course the place everybody asks about first. The shithouse, as we affectionately call it. I'm afraid the indoor plumbing is still for guests only.

Hal's first day ended with a lesson on the arcane science of the diamond hitch.

—That's more like the Gordian knot, son. Here, let me show you.

Trask had his doubts about Rawson. For the past two years the young man had been living in England. Last year, at the age of twenty-one, he had published a book of poetry, *Empty and Waste is the Sea,* a book that Trask hadn't read, but that he heard had gained a modest fame both in Canada and across the

Atlantic. Somewhere, this ethereal type had learned to ride, passably, and aim a rifle, and if that awkward shyness left him he could charm the ladies. What he didn't know about trail life and packhorses young O'Hagan and the other guides could teach him.

As it was now, they rode circles around him and delighted in the fact.

—I took a poet on a packtrip a few years back, Trask said to Hal the first day. Well, he was a painter and poet, that's what he called himself. He told me his god was Nature. I thought to myself, We'll see about that. When we set up camp the first night he took a stick and scraped himself a little trench around his tent and pissed in it. I said, why the holy circle? And he informed me, quite seriously, that it would keep away the bears. So I told him it was a rare pleasure to meet a god-fearing man.

24

While Rawson waits below in the camp, Byrne climbs the glacier. He stops to rest against a boulder lying in the middle of the ice, blows on his cold fingers, and writes in his notebook.

There can be little doubt the glacier is at present retreating. The terminus is an arcuate, shelf-like lip, furrowed with the longitudinal depressions of seasonal ice wasting. The frontal slope varies between 20 and 30 degrees, and this fluctuation also indicates the glacier's unstable state. The logical next step is to determine as closely as possible the flow rate and the average yearly amount of recession.

Collie's Geographical Society report, meticulous as the man himself, noted that Byrne's accident occurred at the base of the first icefall. Several metres from a large dome of rock, a *nunatak* as the Inuit named these solitary landmarks in a desert of ice. Collie remembered the nunatak as a marker of the farthest point reached by the expedition before Byrne's mishap. Its dark, humpbacked shape is visible from the chalet.

In Europe they are called rognons, *but here the Native word, its harsh sound, seems more accurate.*

The nunatak is huge. Byrne circumnavigates it, finds a shred of faded green cloth in a crevice of the rock. He was wearing a green scarf the day of his fall into the crevasse. He knows that Collie removed it to examine him.

He takes his bearings from the nunatak, marches several paces down the glacier surface. At the time of his fall, the blue ice was bare and glazed with meltwater. Now there is a light dusting of fresh snow, but not enough to hide crevasses. There are none as far as he can see around him, and he admits to himself the foolishness of his search. The chasm into which he fell was no doubt long ago sealed up by the forward flow of the glacier.

25

He reaches the base of the first icefall. He can walk no farther, and now must climb.

The glass mountain.

He takes the newly-purchased gear from his rucksack, straps the claws onto his boots. Steps out of the sunlight into the icefall's colder penumbra.

The point of his axe bites through the brittle surface, into the harder layers beneath. He gouges the ice with his lobster claws, hauls himself upward, carefully planning each movement, no matter how slight. The dagger technique. Stab with the axe, the boot, crawl upward like a slow and methodical spider. Breathing in deeply, breathing out slowly.

An ice shard skitters from above, bounces off his coat sleeve and nicks his cheek just below the eye. A larger chunk falls past him. He presses himself flat against the wall, holds his breath, listens.

Silence.

26

After an hour the sun has risen overhead and climbs with him, now an enemy. The ice weakens, sloughs off its brittle outer skin, releasing itself into liquid all around him. He is climbing an emerging waterfall.

Breathing has become a labour. His arms tire far too quickly, his neck and shoulders are rigid with pain. The broken collarbone that did not heal well has betrayed him. An unexpected weakening of strength, a loss of concentration on this vertical river would be fatal.

He touches his forehead to the ice, closes his eyes. If he makes it to the top of this wall, there is still another trek of over three kilometres to the base of the upper icefall. The true terra incognita. And only beyond that obstacle will he finally reach the névé.

It might as well be the moon.

He drags himself into camp in late afternoon, huddles in front of the fire while Rawson packs their gear.

27

In the field hospital, Byrne lies stretched on a cot with a hot water bottle pressed against his shoulder, a strip of wet surgical gauze over his face. From the saloon tent a piano rattles out delirious ragtime tunes.

Laughter. The clink of glasses. At the other end of the long tent, behind a white screen, someone is being loudly sick.

The orderly sets down a tray, beef tea in a feeding cup. Byrne sits up, peels off the gauze.

—It was all I could find, doctor.

Byrne nods, takes the cup. The orderly jerks his head toward the far end of the tent.

—The cook spent the day in some drinking hole. That's his penance disturbing your repose.

Byrne lies back against the pillow. His limbs and face throb, throwing off heat. In the cool dusk he is the sun's memory.

The easy slopes of the lower glacier will be the edge of his known world. He will never see the field, never climb from the dark jumbled debris of rock into that space of burning, eternal light.

28

FRANK TRASK'S GUIDED WALKING TOURS

To the alpine meadows and the Arcturus glacier, starting from the chalet lobby at 7:15 a.m. sharp, led by experienced mountaineers who can

*answer all questions. Please consult
beforehand with the management
concerning appropriate dress. All other
supplies, and a luncheon, will be
provided.*

*"We can take you above the clouds at
a very reasonable charge, and let you
touch a real glacier."*

Trask snaps his fingers. He is exuberant, light-hearted.
The new porcelain has arrived on this morning's train.
Just in time for the long-awaited visit by Sibelius, the
railroad's major financier. As the crates are pried
open, Trask, hovering on tiptoe behind the haulers,
breaks into a beatific smile. In the same tone he uses
to calm a horse, he exhorts care from the men, *easy
now with that piece, gently, that's it,* as a gleaming array
of washbasins and commodes is revealed in the raw
air.

He touches the cold porcelain with reverent
hands, as if it were the substance of civilization.

Another crate is unloaded and pried open for
inspection, one full of glass bottles. Another of Trask's
ideas become reality, one he hopes will reveal to
Sibelius his talent for exploiting to the full the
resources at hand.

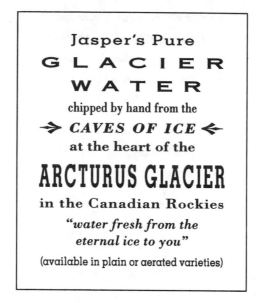

Jasper's Pure

G L A C I E R
W A T E R

chipped by hand from the

→ *CAVES OF ICE* ←

at the heart of the

ARCTURUS GLACIER

in the Canadian Rockies

*"water fresh from the
eternal ice to you"*

(available in plain or aerated varieties)

With the coming of the railroad and the building of the spur line and the chalet, Trask's fortunes
blossomed. He had become a major outfitter and
freighter along the mountain section of the Grand
Trunk. As he liked to say, *the biggest toad in the puddle.*

His one great annoyance was that Sibelius, the
man for whom he was in essence the representative
here, had not yet made a visit. Trask hoped to impress
him with his schemes and plans for improvements,
and at last he gathered the courage to send the railroad
baron a telegram, inviting him to Jasper. After a long
wait, a reply came: *I'll consider any ideas you've got,*

Mr. Trask, but I prefer words on a page. They don't gestic-
ulate. Write it all out before I get there.

29

—The railroad, says Trask, hauled this place out of the
ice age. When I go back east people no longer say to
me *Jasper, where the hell is Jasper?*

Some of the townspeople believe Sleeping Beauty
is their myth. They have been awakened from a frozen
slumber into the warm embrace of the twentieth
century.

Freight trains carrying fabrics and spices from
Asia rocket through the valley, leaving an imagined
perfume of the orient in their wake. Electric lamps line
the main boulevard, not yet paved, it must be admitted, but ladies with parasols and gentlemen in white
suits will soon stroll there.

The days when savage men wrestled with grizzly bears, or were said to have done so, have vanished
in the glow of these electric street lamps. And in this
new age, for good or ill, women attempt fields of
endeavour that were once reserved only for men. Such
as mountain climbing.

—There was that Mary Schaeffer a few years
back, the American woman who says she discovered
Maligne Lake. Well, I can tell you it was one of my

boys, guiding her, that climbed a mountain and saw it first. And now we've got the famous Miss Freya Becker. *Freya.* What kind of a name is that for a Christian soul?

Trask is talking too much and he knows it. This is his first face-to-face encounter with Sibelius, and he is nervous, perspiring, driven by panic to blurt out whatever tumbles through his head. Elspeth, at the far end of the long dining table, looks amused by his discomfort. And Hal Rawson, as usual, says nothing.

Sibelius, having at long last come to see the town he envisioned, sits across from Trask, quietly stroking his Vandyke beard. Trask is surprised to find him a small, unremarkable-looking man. He thinks that if Sibelius had been the beefy, cigar-chomping capitalist he had imagined, the evening would be going much more smoothly. He would know what to say. He would not be making this flustered attempt to fill the silence with words, like a fireman shoveling coal to feed a dying locomotive engine.

—Anyhow, Trask says, it seems likely Miss Becker is a devotee of Sappho, if you catch my meaning. So perhaps she doesn't count as a representative of womanhood.

Sibelius frowns. Then it hits Trask like a stomach punch: Sibelius and Freya's father were business acquaintances.

—The private affairs of Miss Becker, Sibelius says at last, will be discussed no further in my presence.

—Well, you know I was only repeating the kind of gossip that runs rampant in a place like this, where people don't know each other very well.

—That'll be enough, Mister Trask. Now I want you to show me the town we've built.

30

On the map in his Montreal office, a red X marked the site of the city Anton Sibelius had planned. A railroad and a city in the mountains, to rival and surpass the domain of the Canadian Pacific to the south.

As a young clerk in the Hudson's Bay Company he had seen a painting at the Fort Garry headquarters: Gentle green hills around a placid lake. Peaceable Natives camped in the shade of giant trees. And far in the distance a mountain peak, weightless, serene, from which a fragile glacier wound a serpentine course. In the bright morning sunlight the avenues and spires of ice shone in the air like a celestial city.

A city amid the ice.

Trains carrying away the black diamonds of coal to a world hungry for energy. Trains disgorging fresh adventurers before a domed and turreted hotel.

Trains with refrigerator cars, packed with glacier ice, so that travelling dignitaries could dine on fresh lobster as they rushed across the plains, hundreds of miles from the ocean.

31

Nothing is said, but something is clearly troubling Sibelius. At the end of the tour he returns to his private rail car, and Trask goes with him. They head west, out of town, in silence.

Several miles out the whistle blasts a warning as the line crosses a trestle bridge over a gorge. Trask watches the baron's sallow face for a raised eyebrow, the slightest twitch, any reaction to the sudden terrifying view, one that has made many passengers gasp, cover their eyes, even faint.

To Trask's horror, Sibelius signals for a halt on the far side of the bridge. Brakes squeal and cutlery clatters in the dining car.

The baron climbs down from the train and walks swiftly to the edge of the gorge, whipping a silk handkerchief out of his breastpocket to wipe his glistening brow. Trask scrambles after him.

—Do you see this? Sibelius says in a tremulous whisper. He points to a stunted spruce that the wind has almost uprooted from its foothold at the edge of the gorge. The tree leans out over the abyss, gnarled, like a tortured soul on the verge of a final leap.

—Unsightly, Sibelius mutters, shaking his head. He bends down, grasps the trunk and is pulled off balance, his polished black oxfords slipping on the wet stone. Trask lunges forward and grips his arm.

—And dangerous.

32

Hal Rawson returns to the chalet bunkhouse in the evening after the reception for Sibelius. He takes off the ill-fitting suit and slips into a flannel shirt and wool trousers.

Pain twinges in his right hand. He holds it up, examines the bright red bead growing beside his thumbnail. He tore skin from his dry, calloused fingers all through the reception, under the edge of the tablecloth. Removing himself from the tedium in strips.

From the pile of books in his steamer trunk he picks out Housman's *A Shropshire Lad,* props a pillow, and stretches out on the bed.

The green fields of England. He lived in London for two years with his uncle. Hardly looked at the countryside. Too busy trying to live as he thought a writer should. Bohemian. Scrambling around in a panic to meet literary eminences and women, impress them with his serious writerliness. He knows that people often thought him to be English. There were times when he found it useful or just amusing to affect the clipped accent of the poets and lecturers he often went to hear.

He likes to read aloud, when alone, in mimicry of those grave, resonant voices.

Loveliest of trees the cherry now. . . .

He is suddenly aware of the sounds and smells around him in this bunkhouse. The sharp tang of spruce, kerosene, the blankets with their faint, indelible reek of smoke. The nickering of horses in the corral.

He looks down at himself, his clothing, sees an actor in a wild west show.

33

Celeste, one of Elspeth's chambermaids, is in love with him.

Elspeth watches her. This girl is a long way from her home town. Nervous, forgetful, often cries at night, the other girls have told her. Has to be cautioned about chewing her fingernails, as it is unsightly to the guests. And now she is in love.

At the chalet staff picnic, Hal sat with Celeste

on the green sloping bank of Lac Beauvert. He quoted
Yeats, his favourite poet.

> *She carries in the candles,*
> *And lights the curtained room,*
> *Shy in the doorway*
> *And shy in the gloom;*
>
> *And shy as a rabbit,*
> *Helpful and shy,*
> *To an isle in the water*
> *With her I would fly.*

Then a woman shouted Hal's name, and he
jerked to his feet like a marionette. She was a stranger
to Celeste, this thin, quick young woman with
cropped blond hair. She *pounced* on Hal and gave
Celeste a quick, cold glance.

Hal gave a helpless shrug as he was led away.

Now Celeste sees him only from a distance,
always in the company of that strange woman, Freya
Becker. The scandalous lady alpinist, some have
dubbed her, or the bitch who wears men's trousers.
What's worse, she's older than Hal. Her face is ruddy,
prematurely lined by wind and sun, but her eyes are a
beautiful, watery green.

34

Freya made a special demand for Rawson this summer. *Unlike the rest of your crew*, she grinned at Trask, *he speaks*. Rawson helps her gather supplies and choose packhorses.

At first it is her language that shocks him. The way her words push him into an unfamiliar room, spin him around. She tells stories from her travels, stories he finds difficult to believe.

—I'm not sure, but I think I killed a man, on a lake near Chojend.

—Chojend. Where is that?

—Exactly. It's a city north of the Hindu Kush. The ancient name was Alexandria the Farthest. The locals have a legend about its founding.

—Never mind the legend. What about the man?

—Someone climbed aboard our houseboat. He was standing in the cabin doorway, there was a gauze curtain and I couldn't see if he had a weapon. My host said shoot and I did and he disappeared. A few seconds later we heard a splash. He was a thief, the others said, they kill.

—So you did the right thing.

—That's what they told me. I don't know. I'm more angry now for what happened when I got home. I did a piece about Chojend for the paper, and the

editor talked me into dropping that part of the story.
I gave in to him.

35

He watches the way her body moves beneath the
rough male disguise. When she tugs at a saddle strap,
or heaves a satchel of climbing equipment over her
shoulder. The muscles as loose and supple as water,
then pulling taut. A decisive body. The truth of her
stories is revealed there.

They hike out together from the chalet, along
Jonah Creek into the high alpine tundra. On either side
of them the mountain walls are laden with cirque glaciers. They are walking through a hall of frozen kings.

—All this wasted light, Freya says. I didn't
bring the camera.

They find a place to set up camp in the open
meadow, where a rivulet of the creek spills half-hidden
through the thick carpet of moss.

36

They spend the day hiking and return to camp in the
evening.

—Hungry?

—Starving.

Hal starts a fire and unpacks his cooking supplies.

—What's on the menu?

—Whitefish, rice, tinned vegetables. And some hot cocoa for dessert.

Freya sets up her tent and crawls inside to change her clothes. She comes back out in an olive-green wool sweater and a white culotte, then notices his amazed stare.

—What?

—Sorry.

She sits down across the fire from him.

—At the lake the other day, was that your sweetheart?

—Celeste? No.

—She was pretty. And the look she gave me. Daggers.

—Well, I'd just been reciting a poem. You interrupted us in the middle of Yeats.

—I take it poetry has a use then.

37

After supper Hal shakes his own tent loose from its canvas sack.

—You don't need that, Freya says.

He finds he is not shocked to be making love with her. What surprises him is her unexpected gentleness. He is almost asleep when he feels the touch of her finger tracing letters on his arm. *I love you.*

—You can't, he whispers. Not yet.

—Write it and see, she says. On me.

38

In the morning they linger together in the tent.

—How about a quick splash in the creek.

—Freya, that water's arctic.

—I'm going. See you later.

She crawls out of the tent and he stays behind, thinking it's too late to come out after her, like an adoring dog chasing her heels. He watches through the open tent flap as her slender, pale body disappears down the green meadow. He lies back on the blankets and closes his eyes, hears a splash and her shriek.

—Yow!

She laughs, calls out to him, but the wind carries the words away. He lies still, sunlight pulsing red on his eyelids. He imagines he is in a tent on the edge of a desert of sand.

She comes back in like the sun, her face burning. But when she moves into his arms her body is ice.

—There, now *I'm* arctic.

He watches her sleep. She stirs and water slips from her wet hair, into the cup of flesh between neck and collarbone. He touches the droplet with a finger and she opens her eyes.

39

—I was worried when I found out you were a poet.

—Why?

—I don't care much for poetry, for one thing. But I was more afraid you'd keep me up all night talking about the infinite, the ineffable, the *truth*.

—That's been your experience of poets?

—Yes. Your quote at the glasshouse was a good example of what I mean.

—I'm not a poet.

—What about your book?

—I haven't written anything in months. When I saw my words in print I wanted to run away and hide. Maybe that's why I ended up here.

—What was wrong with your words?

—One poem described a lizard crawling across a mirror, but it was just a symbol. Of what? I can't even remember. It was an idea, I hadn't actually seen it. In other poems I used words like *lute* and *arbalest*. I realized I'd written about nothing that I'd lived through. None of it was my life, my experience.

—Words always do that to me, even when I'm reporting what we like to call the facts. I think to myself, was that really what I saw, what I felt? But I keep trying, I have to try to nail things down with the exact words, and sometimes I feel I've come close. That's the reward. To feel that nail go in and hold something.

—I'll try not to mention the infinite, or the ineffable.

—Good.

—If I do, just put your hand here. Or here. And I won't say a word.

40

—I'm here in Jasper, Freya says, for the same reason I've been to Asia and Egypt and Mexico.

—And what's that?

—Too many fathers.

Something happened to her father when she was a young girl. No one ever told her exactly what it was, but she was patient, she watched and listened. From her mother's rare but bitter accusations, her father's whisky-soaked mutterings, she put together a story.

—He was a tireless adulterer, but I think he became too good at it. He had to keep trying for greater challenges, bigger trophies. And then he met his match. I don't know who the woman was, I think she might have been Greek, I'm not sure. But I always wished I could meet her. She must have been the Queen of Swords.

Freya remembers his longest absence, at least half a year. She celebrated her ninth birthday without him. And then everyone—her mother, her uncles—said he was going to be with them again very soon. But they weren't excited about his return the way they used to be, when they would bustle around the house as if it were an office building, shouting at each other down the hallways about the way something or some-one was going to be put back on track now that George was coming home. This time they huddled together in the big empty dining room and whispered, it seemed to Freya, like frightened mice.

—When I think of the day we went to meet his train, I have this image of him stepping from different compartments at the same time. Of course I didn't realize it until he'd been back at home for a while, but he was split, in pieces. It was terrifying, so I made it into a kind of game, a joke. As if some insane labora-tory experiment had done this to him, fractionated him, and I could classify the various George Beckers. My amazing collection of fathers.

First there was the earth father, the brute. The one who could barely feed himself on bad days.

—He brought home a tin of cookies for me once. When he walked in the door I knew which of my fathers this was, so I just sat there, not sure what to do or say. He tried to talk to me and I just stared at the wall. Then he started throwing the cookies at me. Hard.

Hurts, doesn't it, he said. *Get used to it.*

Then there were the various opaque, fleeting fathers. The ones who would appear suddenly in the morning, in their housecoats, wolf down a breakfast and talk on and on about their latest grand scheme. One of these George Beckers was mostly electricity. He read a lot, and paced around the rest of the time, chewing his nails, drumming his fingers on the windowpane as he gazed out at the street. Another, the one her mother went to bed with, was sort of thin and papery. For a while these fathers could fool Freya into thinking *he's back, this is him, all of him together again.* But the plans and schemes rarely succeeded the way they had in the past, and then these doubtful, wavering fathers quickly faded away.

It was the water father that Freya loved.

—He was quick, he danced. I thought his laugh was like water falling. I loved to dance for him, put on little performances. I could make him laugh, and then I'd feel that cool, gentle water wash over me.

—He took me to a carnival once. We went on a Ferris wheel. I remember feeling foolish on this thing, ashamed of the cheap deception. It was supposed to be like flying, but it just went around and around, showing you the same sights over and over again. A fence plastered with bills. Some kid's mother waving up at him. The bored ride operator looking at the women's legs. And the fence again, and around we go.

—That was the day I knew I had to leave. And I didn't hide the fact, at least not from *him*. When I was seventeen he helped me get my own apartment. Freya's first scandal, a schoolgirl living on her own. This was Montreal, not Paris. I had to admit it, without him I probably would've been stuck doing something safe and ladylike for the rest of my life. I hated myself for needing George Becker's money and influence, so I kept this thought in mind: it was *him*, the water father, he gave me my freedom, not any of the others.

One by one, over the years, her pantheon of fathers dwindled. Perhaps, she thought, the stronger ones killed the weak. She used to believe the brute would live the longest, he seemed indestructible, but the only father left now is the one made of air.

—He's invisible, she says, but sometimes I can feel him hovering over me, it doesn't matter how far away I get.

41

She tells him about the Slovak woman who lived in the apartment next to hers.

—Sophie was reading *Dracula,* and she got it

into her head that I was a vampire. After we became friends we had a great laugh about it, the way I looked to her. How I would be holed up all day in my room, and appear only in the evening, pale and twitchy. I was always asking about everybody else in the building, which she thought made good sense if I was hunting for potential victims or watching out for my enemies. But the biggest clue was, whenever Sophie mentioned God or church or heaven, she said I would get this pained grimace on my face. Then she found out I wasn't a vampire, I was a writer.

—Trask thinks that you're, well, a lover of women.

—Is that right. And what do you think?

—I had a dream about it. About you and a woman. Together.

—Who was it?

—I can't tell you. Not in the cold light of day. It wouldn't come out right.

—It must have been quite the dream. Were you in it?

—Well, I was watching.

—I'm sure you were.

—I mean I was watching a dream. I was dreaming it. There was a man there, though, but I couldn't see who it was.

—Who was the woman? Tell me, damn it.

—No.

42

Celeste has been sent home.

—I heard a kettle whistling and I found her in the front parlour, Elspeth tells Byrne.

Four o'clock in the morning. Sitting at the window, a tray of tea, orange marmalade, and biscuits on the table beside her.

Celeste smiled at Elspeth, raised a tea cup to her lips, and bit a piece out of it.

43

—I just want to look at you tonight.

—That's all?

—I can't believe you killed someone.

—I told you, I'm not sure I did. But I don't think it leaves a scar.

—Your feet.

She laughs.

—What?

—Look at your feet. Every part of you is so . . . charming.

—Oh my God.

—I can't think of a better word. Maybe it's not just the meaning. It's the letters, too. The letters of the word *charming*.

—In bold face at least?

—No, italic.

44

Byrne is reviewing charts in the hospital tent when Swift appears at his side. No, the American growls impatiently, he isn't in need of any medical attention. And he never will be.

—I heard your name mentioned when the surveyors stopped at my place, and I thought, now there's a man with some sense.

He leans in closer to Byrne.

—I thought you might know something about the situation here. They were supposed to make me an offer, for my land.

—Who?

—The Lords of the Iron Horse. The bastards skirted my property line by a few hundred yards. Because I reported their surveyors for poaching. And they damn well were.

Swift's homestead claim was inviolable because he had filed for it years before. The land was his. He had built on it, improved it, saved it from destruction by the forces of nature. After much deliberation by the officials in charge of the new park, he had been allowed to remain when the other settlers were ushered out, and given the titles of honourary game warden and fire-ranger.

His solitary empire was at an end, but he had vowed to make sure they paid him handsomely for it. The proposed railroad was to come up the valley along the surveyed route. The line would have to pass through his property, raising its value beyond his capacity to calculate.

Realizing this, he wrote to a well-known financier in the east, told him of his expected profit. Months later, to his surprise, a letter of reply reached him. The financier was interested. He had consulted with Sibelius and the survey crews. Swift's land was perfectly situated.

Together they envisioned a sprawling complex of rustic resort cabins, tennis courts, terraced slopes, swimming pools. And a name: Swiftmere.

—He sent me these letters, you should've seen them, on creamy vellum paper. And now, well, the letters are all dry and yellow, and he never appeared in the flesh.

Swift wants to know if Byrne has heard anything of him.

—I'm asking you because I don't trust the others. Never get a straight answer from any of them.

Swift whispers the financier's name. Byrne knows it, having read in the papers of his grandiose plans for developing the west. Recently the papers also listed him as one of the dignitaries lost on the maiden voyage of the *Titanic.*

If Swift is crushed by the news, he does not show it. From Little Bighorn to the *Titanic,* thinks Byrne. Swift has lived a life at the edge of disasters. No wonder he went looking for an empty valley.

Swift shrugs.

—Well, I'll be here, 'til doomsday. The barons had their chance. Now I'm going to sit in the middle of their pretty park like a rusty spike.

He allows himself a grey smile.

—Come out to my place tomorrow, for dinner. We're not fancy, but you'll get a good meal.

—I was wondering about Sara's people, Byrne finally dares to ask. From the Arcturus settlement, the ones who took care of me after I fell in the crevasse.

Instead of fading, Swift's smile grows enigmatically wider.

—Most of them scattered. West over the pass, north into the Smoky country. Nobody kept track.

—Sara as well, I suppose. You don't know where she might be now?

—I have a pretty good idea. She's at the house, probably standing on the porch wondering where in the hell I am.

—I didn't know, Byrne stammers. I mean to say, when I first met her, I thought she lived alone.

—She did, then, no matter what I argued to the contrary. There was no way she was coming down from her icy stronghold just to please me. Only when the government so very kindly told her to vacate, she had to decide. Leave the mountains altogether, or move in with me. That was it.

He strokes his grizzled moustache.

—I'm still a bit surprised at her choice.

45

When they pull up at the house in Swift's pony trap, Sara steps out onto the porch.

Her hair is white. That surprises him. If he was right about her age when he first met her, she cannot now be much over forty. The image in his memory has not changed with time, he realizes, and he wonders if he looks the same way to her, familiar and yet strange.

—Once again I am your guest, he says lightly, and sees by the quick nod of her head that this time she will not be so welcoming. He imagines he can understand the reason. The railroad that carried him back here also brought the surveyors and work crews who built the chalet, and who tore down the trading post, as Swift has just told him, to build a raft to ferry themselves across Arcturus Creek.

—It's Doctor Byrne, Swift says, with a note of anger in his voice at Sara's impassive silence.

—I know.

A girl of about eight or nine, in a white sack dress and sandals, appears beside her at the door.

—And this is Louisa.

The girl will not look at Byrne. She kicks off her sandals, jumps from the porch and scampers across the yard.

—The child can't sit still, Swift says.

—I'm used to that, Byrne says. Children and doctors are natural enemies.

During dinner and afterwards on the porch, Sara says very little. Louisa sits at her feet, holding the skein of wool she is winding. It is Swift who does the storytelling.

—When I first came to this valley, he says, I found an arm.

He was in the heart of a spruce bog, surrounded by crooked, black trees. His ox was stuck. The huge animal thrashed for a moment in the thick green pool and then went still, its flanks steaming in the cool air. Swift stood back at a distance, more wary of this great bulk becalmed than he had been of the ox's frequent displays of temper. He shook his head.

—I turned away, thinking this was the end of line, and then I saw it.

An arm sticking up out of the spongy brown

earth. A bloodless arm in a tattered sleeve of black cloth. The hand, bone white, clutched a survey stake. Swift pried the stake out of the hand's dry grasp and checked its number. It was the one indicated on his map. This was the land he had filed for.

Somehow, after a desperately long time, the ox hauled itself out onto firmer ground. Swift approached, righted his belongings on the cart, and went on.

Byrne shakes his head.

—Forgive me if I'm a bit incredulous.

Swift scowls.

—It's hanging on the wall, he says, gripping the arms of his chair. The stake, I mean. I can go get it for you right now.

—It's not the stake I have doubts about.

—Well, you may be the doctor, but. . . .

—Let's have the story, Sara says.

Swift took the stake with him, slung in his belt. Up the valley of the Athabasca, until the survey stakes ran out and he lost sight of the river.

He pushed through a dense thicket of willows that scratched his face and tore at the canvas on his cart. A wheel jammed in the crevice of a split stone. Swift knelt to free it, growling soft curses. Then he stood up, listened. A gust of cool air stirred the leaves around him.

He knew then there was an open space just beyond the next stand of willows. The sound and smell of flowing water reached him. He stepped from the thick brush into an open meadow by the river.

Into the midst of a herd of wild horses.

Swift stood motionless. The horses raised their heads from the grass they were feeding on and watched him. Their quiet shapes, grey and paint and roan, stood gathered in the clearing like suddenly remembered dreams. Slowly, led by a dappled mare, the horses turned and moved away, down the long stretch of open meadow.

Swift glanced around, turning where he stood. He knelt and drove the stake into the earth.

46

When he had built a sod-roofed hut, Swift went exploring further up the Athabasca valley. He had seen a frayed rope around the neck of one of the horses.

He found a cabin and a fire burning nearby, with a black pot suspended over it from a tripod of aspen poles. He lifted the lid of the pot. Three skinned rabbits, eyes gaping, turning in the bubbling water. Swift grinned and nodded his head.

He heard a shout and looked up. A group of women were walking towards him across the clearing. One of them raised her hand and waved to him. Her voice, with its unmistakable English accent, rang like a bell through the still air.

Swift shouldered his axe and stalked away.

The next day a welcoming committee of men came to Swift's cabin. Albert Blackbird and his four sons. They asked him if he was planning to stay and he said he was.

How many people live in this valley? Swift asked them.

Seven families here, by the Athabasca, Albert Blackbird said. *And five further up, at the river's source.*

What about the Englishwoman?

Blackbird shook his head.

There haven't been any English here for years.

47

His cabin was finished. By the next summer he had broken land and planted wheat.

He knelt one bright morning at the edge of his field and put his hand close to the earth. Felt a cool rivulet of air being sucked along, as though a giant were drawing breath.

The fire appeared on the crest of the bare hill.

Smoke dragged behind the rushing flames like a grey cape. The wild grasses exploded into black ash as the heat roared over them.

The other men in the valley gathered at Swift's, shouting to each other through the thickening smoke. One man rode up in a hay wagon, reining in his two frantic draft horses. The others waved at him, pointed over his head and he turned, saw the burden of fire he was carrying to them. The man jumped down and unhitched the horses. He took hold of their bridles, jerked their heads in the direction of the river, and slapped their flanks to start them galloping. Behind him the burning wagon disappeared in its own smoke.

Most of the women had gone down to the river with the children, although some came to help fight the fire.

It never stops burning, Albert Blackbird told Swift. *Just hides underground for a few years.*

They fought the fire for the rest of that day and into the night. Swift was seen wherever the flames were the most threatening, his shovel flying. They fought for three days and nights, resting when the many smaller fires seemed to be vanquished, digging furiously wherever they leapt to life again.

On the morning of the third day, people from Arcturus Creek appeared on horseback. Sara was with them. They had wakened the day before to ash falling like grey snow and had come to offer their help.

That night the fire fighters could see a constellation of livid embers in the blackness around their fields. They remained watchful.

At midday a grey twilight hung over the valley, and from it rain began to fall. The charred land steamed and hissed. The Blackbird brothers, the Miettes, Finlay and his wife Mistaya, and Sara gathered around the place where Swift stood, pouring water from a leather flask over his head.

Too exhausted to celebrate, they sat down together on the bare earth and looked into one another's smoke-blackened faces without recognition.

Swift looked across at Sara, who was sitting crouched forward, holding a wet cloth to her face.

You are the Englishwoman? he said.

Sara stared at him, and understanding slowly dawned. The day, last summer, she had been visiting her friends the Blackbirds at their cabin and had called out to him across the clearing. He had been fooled by her voice.

Yes, I am.

Swift nodded, his face twisting into a grimace that could have been an answering smile.

You did well.

The others laughed, and Swift soon realized his mistake.

Well I'm damned.

When Sara got up to leave she stumbled and

fell to the ground. Swift's cabin was the nearest. He helped her to walk there, sat her down and gave her a tin mugful of water. Then he cooked a meal of fried bread and potatoes.

It's not my own bread, he said. *Not yet.*

While she ate he stood at the open doorway squinting out into the dusk. When she was finished he said, *I've still got some work.*

He placed a heavy black phonograph record on the Victrola, the tenor John Parkinson singing "*Che gelida manina*" from Puccini's *La Bohème*. He asked Sara to play it again when it ended, and to keep playing it until he returned.

He took a shovel and went out. In the dark he was able to find the last of the embers, invisible in daylight, and smother them in earth.

The smoke surrounded him, burned his eyes. He put a wet rag over his nose and mouth. Found his way back to the cabin by the sound of the tenor's voice.

48

—It was the only music I owned, he tells Byrne. Other than my bugle, which doesn't get much use out here. I wore that Parkinson record out long ago. There've been a few fires over the years.

Swift creakily hums the melody. He shuts his eyes, settles back in his chair, and folds his arms with finality across his chest. The story is at an end, and the evening as well. Sara offers to take Byrne to town in the pony trap.

—Nonsense, I'll walk. After all, it's so late.

—The pony knows the way, and old people like me sleep like owls, with one eye open.

—I didn't mean to imply. . . .

—Hop up.

—Thank you.

—Are you coming with us, Louisa?

The girl nods and scrambles up into the trap between them. Swift wakes up, mutters a good night.

After they have driven for some distance in silence, Byrne says,

—About the arm, holding the spike. You believe him?

—Yes, the girl says sleepily. Sara puts an arm around her.

—There's your answer.

—I suppose it is. And really I'm not one who should be doubting the fabulous tales of others.

—I know, Sara says.

Byrne stares straight ahead.

—You know.

—Not everything.

—But you understand what brought me back here.

—Some of it.

—What?

—You looked about this pale the night they brought you to the cabin.

He turns. Her grey eyes hold him.

—You were feverish, and you babbled a fair bit.

—What about? He glances at the girl. Tell me, Sara, what did I say?

—Enough that I could guess we might see you again. That there was something here you wouldn't forget. You'd have to come back and try to finish the story.

They drive in silence around the bend of the dark hill. The lights of Jasper flicker through the trees.

—Can I finish it? Byrne finally asks.

—I don't know everything, but I know it's a story with wings, Sara says. They're hard to catch.

49

An early September snowfall brings summer to an end. The chalet road is clogged with slush, creviced with wheel-ruts. But on the morning of Byrne's departure the sun is shining again. The breeze from the west is warm.

He searches for Elspeth at the chalet, to say goodbye. She is not there.

—She asked for the day off, Trask says. I nearly fell out of my chair.

—She didn't say where she'd be?

—No, but I can give her your regards, if that's what you want. You're going now, I take it? Because the morning run into town is pulling out in ten minutes.

—No, I'm not leaving until later today.

By midafternoon the snow is gone. The sky is cloudless. Byrne gazes across the valley at Arcturus glacier, its blue ice bare and gleaming again.

In the evening he meets Elspeth stepping from the chalet train.

—I thought I'd missed you, she says. Freya and Hal took me hiking with them. Are you leaving now?

—No, Byrne says. I've decided to stay one more week.

50

Freya. Her history. Hal understands that for all her confidence she walks a tightrope. She runs, leaps, pulls her daredevil stunts over an abyss like the one that dashed her father to pieces. And he stumbles along behind her. She needs no help from him. If he gets too close he will only throw off her sense of balance.

She crouches with her back to him on the gravel shore of the river, working with her camera. He tells her he might visit his parents this winter.

—Where do they live? she asks without looking at him.

—They're divorced. My father hides out in his cottage on the Ottawa River. He makes furniture. My mother is remarried, in Toronto.

She is silent for a moment, then turns to face him.

—I'm leaving at the end of the week, she says.

—You should start packing then.

—No, there's plenty of time for that. I don't bring much with me.

51

Hal goes with Freya to the station, helps with her baggage, and then stands in the crowded waiting hall, avoiding her eyes.

—Say something, Hal.

—Don't leave.

—We talked about it. I'm coming back next spring.

—Yes, I know.

—This is not how I wanted to say goodbye.

—I don't think it can be helped.

In the station, waiting for her train out of Jasper, Freya glimpses Byrne as she passes the gentlemen's smoking room. At least she thinks it might be the doctor. She stops, takes a backward step. She can see only the back of his head, his shoulders. One hand holding an open book.

She steps forward, then hesitates. The one man in this town she's not sure how to approach.

The man that might be Byrne rises abruptly and walks out the far door. Freya waits a moment longer, then enters the room filled with blue smoke and men. Heads dart up from behind newspapers, eyes follow her. A lioness passing through the room, surefooted, indifferent to lesser powers.

She pauses to glance down at the open book left on the table.

Swedenborg's *The True Christian Religion*. Freya wrinkles her nose. Lunatic theosophist stuff. She'd had it propounded to her by melancholy, bejewelled women at her father's dinner parties. Her eyes take in just a few words before she moves past the table.

—*wonderful it is that each one of that great host, in whichever direction he turns his body and his gaze, beholds the Lord in front of him.*

As she turns back to the main hall she knows it was Byrne.

❋

Elspeth

The snow is almost gone from the grounds.

Frank is expecting great crowds this year. The Grand Trunk has been advertising all over the continent, but despite the warm weather the hotel is still practically empty. So lately I've found a lot more time for the glasshouse. I was there tending to things most of yesterday. Hal kindly risked his neck on a ladder to help me clean the dust and leaves off the roof panes. After that I worked among the plants alone, repotting, watering, planting new bulbs, with all this glorious sunlight streaming in. I'd forgotten that on good days this place can be close to paradise.

In the afternoon I took a rake to the lawn around the outside of the glasshouse. It's the caretaker's job, but I love raking the grass in the spring, when it's still yellow and matted, just beginning to breathe again. When I drag the rake over the grass it seems to purr, like a cat getting its back scratched.

The truth is I've been hiding out in the glasshouse. Ned Byrne has been here for three days now. He's back for the summer, as he said he would be, but not as a railway doctor. He brought a crate of supplies with him, and he says he's going to spend his summer exploring the icefield. I said I hoped he'd come visit us at the chalet once in a while.

God, I've really turned into a wilting flower. ❋

NUNATAK

1

Prismatic compass. Clinometre. Steel tape for baseline measures. Red paint for marking fixed stations.

Byrne cracks open a new notebook. *24 May 1912.*

By calculating flow rate, one should be able to predict the approximate time it would take an object imbedded at a particular location in the ice to travel to the terminus and melt out.

He places a line of stones across the ice surface, stretching from one lateral moraine to the other. Every week he returns and checks the alignment of the stones, with reference to painted boulders on the moraines. A table in his notebook slowly fills with numbers.

2

In the notebook he also sets down his observations.

The branches of the trees near the terminus all grow to one side of the trunk, away from the knife wind blowing off the ice. Ragged pennants.

~

Stones, fragments of a lost continent, lie scattered in the dirty snow of the till plain. A shattered palette at my feet, the mad artist having just stalked away. Grey breccia flecked with acid green and primrose yellow. Pock-marked slabs into which powder of burnt sienna has been ground. The many-coloured constellations of lichen growth: rocks splattered with alizarin crimson and cadmium orange. The purple and white veins of limestone.

The enchantment of these mute fragments is unde-

niable. The bewitching garden of signs. Down among the cool stones, one might not perceive the burning rays of sunlight reflected from lingering patches of summer snow, until it is too late.

~

In certain rare conditions of wind and sunlight, glacial ice evaporates immediately, without passing through the liquid stage. This is called sublimation, a more refined form of melting.

The phenomenon is often accompanied by a rhythmic crackling sound, as if invisible feet were stepping across the ice.

3

Freya leaps. She arrows into the water, slips beneath the broken surface. Her body ripples and recedes, a flickering tongue of flame.

Elspeth watches her from the steps in the shallow end of the pool. She knows that Freya and Hal swim here, naked, late at night. And she knows she should put a stop to it, before they are seen by guests and Trask finds out. But Freya has won her over, captivated her as she has Hal. Ned Byrne, as well, though he pretends otherwise. And Freya is aware of it. Elspeth has felt the ripple of uneasy attraction that passes between the two of them when they are together in a room. Like two solitary wolves aware of one another across a clearing, both keeping the unknown animal in sight at a respectful distance.

Freya's sleek head rises from the dark surface of the water, her ruddy face and pale shoulders steaming in the cool night air. She smiles, wading toward Elspeth.

—You were right, this is heavenly.

4

The sun here sends forth billowing streamers and scintillant curtains of radiance. On the earth this light acts strangely: it has substance, life: it bobs, spills, dances, changes direction. It appears and disappears suddenly, changing the colour and shape of objects in front of your eyes.

~

An exposed ice surface often displays a dull, undifferentiated façade. The intricate crystalline structure can be revealed, however, by pouring a warm liquid over the ice. Urine is the most readily available reagent for this purpose. It will seep into the spaces between the crystals and disassociate them briefly, long enough for the pattern of formation to be examined.

~

The mud at the glacier terminus has a consistency similar to quicksand. You step carefully from one exposed rock surface to another.

The mud swallows boots, as I discovered yesterday. Elspeth was amused to see me limping up to the chalet with one bare foot.

5

Byrne reads the glacier's writing.

Tiny fragments of hard quartz, frozen to the basal surface of the glacier, scar the limestone bedrock as the ice flows forward.

This undersurface, visible from inside an ice cave at the terminus, although smooth in appearance and glossy, like a polished gemstone, is studded with small grains and fragments of rock.

The shiny polish, the fine striations, and irregular chock marks which occur in the underlying bedrock result from contact with this granular ice as it flows.

He makes careful observations of these striation patterns. Crossing the till plain he finds a boulder on which the striations are wavy and realizes it is a petroglyph. Carved by someone in prehistory. A radial series of lines around a central disc. Perhaps a representation of the sun.

Byrne climbs a huge erratic at the edge of the north lateral moraine, finds a river of striations in the rock and follows it. Where the lines submerge underneath the shell of ice there is a labyrinth of scars. They cross and recross the natural markings like a palimpsest. Fossil worm tracks, Byrne thinks, then moves closer.

There are human figures, crude and distorted, but recognizable in various poses: fighting, hunting, giving birth. And other figures, more like animals. Interweaving among the human shapes. And curving lines like the traceries of braided streams. Circles. Arrows. Lines of force.

He traces a frieze along the flank of the cabin-sized boulder.

Confusing everything is the presence of the glacial scars. Undeviating straight lines. They lure his linear mind's eye into following them, away from the human carvings.

The carvings cannot be a history. They do not flow in an orderly sequence. *Who carved them?* he wonders. Sara had said the Snakes once lived in this valley. Athabasca's people.

Following, tracing, taking notes. So that he can avoid leaving the glacier, he makes a cache of food under some morainal rubble and sets up a canvas tent on the till plain. He bathes in a meltwater fall that spills into a shallow rock basin. In the crevices of his wind-hardened face, and along the wings of his nose, every morning he finds and scrubs out fine white powder, rock flour.

While he crouches on the hard clay of a dry rivercourse to eat his pack lunch, he thinks: *If I had no other way to describe what I saw in the crevasse?*

He scratches in the clay with his finger. Sketches a stick figure,

then crosses it out.

Elspeth?

And himself?

6

He invites Rawson to hike up with him and examine the petroglyphs. Perhaps a poet can help him find patterns, identify motifs.

Hal silently runs his hand over the scars in the rock.

—They're strange, wonderful. But I confess I don't understand.

A record of communal memory. Or a prediction. Or both. Or a panorama of visions dreamed in solitude and brushed outside the history of the tribe.

There are no winged figures.

—This may be an alphabet, Hal says. Or a dictionary.

There are many stories. The two of them make summaries, conjectures.

Woman, in a river? Escapes battle, massacre of her people by enemy tribe. Runs away to (from?) forest, lives with rocks, standing stones. The rocks stand in a ring. Erratics? She walks between two of them. Then a space, nothing.

Further along the carving the woman reappears (or is it in fact the same one?) A single line spirals around her. She faces the other way now, west (?), going up into the sun.

The story is there, as far as Byrne can tell, although he knows he and Rawson have created it out of intersecting icons that may not be related.

The images have been here for an unknown length of time, carved into rock the ice had only just scoured and withdrawn from. Not waiting for him to come close and squint at them through his magnifying lens. These scratches have nothing to do with his presence, they do not anticipate him, prophecy him.

7

Among the distinguished visitors to the park this year were Sir Arthur and Lady Conan Doyle and party. They visited a number of points of interest and expressed themselves delighted with everything they saw. Sir Arthur kindly gave his assistance and practical knowledge to the laying out of a nine-hole golf course on a plateau over-

looking Jasper townsite and close to the site of the pro-
posed Grand Trunk Pacific Hotel. He also took a turn at
bat with the local baseball club, and made several excur-
sions to see the sights of our wilderness playground.

Byrne meets the creator of Sherlock Holmes at one of Elspeth's glasshouse receptions. He has heard that Doyle, a doctor, is also a spiritualist, a collector of the unexplained. He offers to take him on a guided trek to the glacier.

Trask grimaces, envisioning wasted time, a broken ankle, bad press.

The two doctors hike slowly across the till plain. Sir Arthur stops often to examine the wildflowers. He marvels at the sky: the change in colour, depth. The purity and sharpness of the air. Byrne takes him to see the rock carvings.

—This is wonderful, Doyle says, taking out a pencil and note pad to make sketches. I may be able to use this.

They carry on across the till plain.

—There, Doyle says, pointing his walking stick at a massive slab of rock perched on a mound of ice, a glacier table.

—Let's stop there.

They circle the glacier table and find a place to climb up. When they reach the flat top of the slab, two small stones roll toward them and wobble to a stop. Doyle chuckles softly.

—The welcoming committee.

They sit down on the slab, open their packs and unwrap sandwiches.

—That young lady at the chalet, Doyle says.

—Elspeth?

—Yes. My wife can sense or see things about certain people. Images that come to her when she is near them, or hears their voices. I don't pretend to understand it, but I have learned not to doubt her gift.

He sips from his water flask.

—She told me that when she shook Elspeth's hand, she had a vision of a tree. A tall pine, green and alive.

He smiles.

—She said she almost sank down and wrapped her arms around the young lady's ankles. She came to her senses in time, thank goodness.

8

Crawling across the gritty snow of the lower glacier, a spider. Doyle sees it first.

—Will you look at that hardy little soul.

Byrne takes a kill jar out of his pack and unscrews the lid.

—I see you come prepared for everything, Doyle says.

Byrne scoops the spider up with a handful of snow and drops it into the jar. He ties a piece of surgical gauze around the rim and stuffs the jar down into his pack.

9

On warm days the volume of meltwater rapidly increases. Rivulets on the glacier surface swell into rushing torrents. Hillocks and banded fonts form on previously level stretches. Passage through this transforming landscape becomes a struggle.

A wide crater-like depression on the glacier slowly fills with water. By early evening it has become a lake, perfectly transparent, filled with the purest water on earth. There are no fish in its depths, no sedges or grasses along the shore. No geese, no shore birds gather here at dusk.

Each night, as the meltwater lessens, the lake subsides. In the morning it has vanished again.

As the glacier flows forward, its topography will inevitably change, and the lake will vanish. For that reason, its ephemerality, I see no reason to give this body of water a name. It will remain the ideal lake.

10

Rawson throws his pack to the ground, takes off his jacket and tosses it on top, kicks off his boots.

Blankets and gear are strewn over the grassy flat, stretched out to dry after the eventful crossing of the Athabasca River. The horses, hazed across the river and now free of their burdens, have trotted out into the meadow. He watches them nip at each other and toss their heads. The tourists from Chicago are gone, having decided to hike the remaining three miles to the chalet rather than wait for Rawson.

He sets the pack contents out around him to survey the damage. The flour is a doughy mass, mixed now with the cocoa powder, and rapidly growing a hard shell. The bannock he had made that morning soggy and limp. He finds the waterproof container of matches, crouches down by the fire pit in his soaked shirt and trousers, shivering.

—Freya, he says aloud. She would be italic, he told her. Now he knows he was thinking of a page of cold text, and in the midst of it, a word that whispers *fire*.

11

Byrne props his notebook on his knees and writes.

I see a rippling pool on the bleached surface of the

nunatak and the sparsity of the landscape draws me to it.
Water.

The pool is perfectly transparent, fringed with a crust of spring ice. Fed by a thin rivulet that spills with the clarity of music from the glacier. I cup my hands and drink.

I lean back on the sun-warmed rock, close my eyes, and listen. The glacier moves forward at a rate of less than one inch every hour. If I could train myself to listen at the same rate, one sound every hour, I would hear the glacier wash up against this rock island, crash like waves, and become water.

12

On the hill above the meadow of flowers floats a silk pavilion. Men and women with glasses of champagne and slices of cake stroll beneath its billowing walls. The members of the alpine club are celebrating the summer's successful climbs.

Rawson leads his string of horses along the edge of the wet meadow, back to the camp. The buzz and shimmer of insects fills the humid sunlit air.

His name is called from across the bright space. He stops. Freya is standing at the pavilion entrance with her camera. She shouts, waves him over. He tethers the lead horse to a tree and climbs the hill. He stops just outside the pavilion, suddenly aware of how he must look. Freya sets her camera down in the grass and steps out of the pavilion to where he is standing as if halted by a spell.

—What happened to you?

—A river.

—You're mud from head to foot.

—Nonsense, darling. Waiter, another bottle of your finest.

She runs a finger lightly down his forehead to the tip of his nose.

—Come to my room tonight, she says, showing him her smudged fingertip. We'll get you clean.

—When will you be finished here?

—I really don't know.

—Are you having a good time?

—You mean me and the other toffs? Yes we are. But there's always a place for poets in our salon.

—I have to go.

—I know. I'll see you.

13

Byrne imagines himself as an alpine Alexander Selkirk, set down here on this island in the ice at his own request. Lying back on a flat slab of limestone, he watches high cirrus clouds form and dissipate.

The sun-heated moisture off the snow rises invisibly and shakes itself out into clouds. Swans. Nana called them the children of Lir.

He remembers Nana telling him the story, how achingly desirable their fate seemed to him as a boy. The enchanted exiles, sundered from home and family, wandering over the dark waters of the earth in immortal loneliness.

Some say they're wandering still, Nana told him. *Until the day God burns up the world with a kiss.*

14

Hal wakes up in her bed. She is not there.

—Freya?

—Here.

She moves across the room, her naked body black against the window for a moment, then invisible and slipping into bed beside him.

—You won't be staying this winter, either.

—No.

—I'm leaving too. I've found a position at the *Herald.* Reporter. They liked the fact that I wrote a book and I can also saddle a horse.

—Hal, you didn't tell me. That's wonderful.

—Is it?

—You'll be busy.

He moves in close to her warmth, slides his arms around her.

—I'd rather spend the winter just like this.

—I get mean and bloodthirsty if I have to stay in one place very long. She bites his wrist. The vampire. You know that.

—And Hal knew his wife Freya and behold, he knew nothing.

—Wife. That's very funny.

—Where will you be?

—You'll laugh, but probably at home with my mother, at least for a while. I can work on my book there.

—You could work on it here. We could hibernate all winter in Elspeth's garden.

—I'm afraid I don't thrive under glass.

15

Hal lights a lamp and sits down on the edge of the bed with a notebook and pen. Freya yawns, opens her eyes.

—What's this?

—I'm going to interview you. An exclusive to the *Herald* by Henry Rawson.

—Fine, I'm too sleepy to argue. Fire away.

—Miss Becker, the readers would like to know how many lovers you've had.

—Mm?

—Miss Becker? Wake up. Please answer the question. How many lovers.

—Two. Next question.

—Two?

—Next question, and then I'm going back to sleep.

—Is there a question you might be willing to answer?

—Ask me what I think I'm doing acting like a man. The other one did.

16

The remains of a shelter built on the nunatak by a group of lost climbers becomes Byrne's scientific observatory. With help from Rawson, he enlarges the rock structure, reinforces it with a wooden framework, a door. They hollow out an area for a fireplace and build a mantle of stones around it. Byrne lines the walls with furs given to him by Sara and Swift, spreads canvas and oilcloth on the floor.

He brings in a camp bed, a pine table, and a chair. He builds shelves and stocks them with books, medical supplies in glass-stoppered bottles, tins of evaporated vegetables, tapers, cooking utensils. He sets a spirit lamp in one wall and a desk clock on the ledge above the fireplace. Next to the clock he places a sea urchin shell, the only surviving relic from his childhood.

When the shelter is completed and stocked, Byrne shuts himself in for his first night. He lights a coal fire, wraps himself in a sleigh blanket, and sits at his table to write by the light of the lamp.

As it grows late the sound of trickling water ceases. The wind has died. He is at the heart of stillness.

The hut is insulated well enough that he is uncomfortable in the blanket, and sloughs it off. He removes his vest and shirt, and his shoes. He writes for a while in his undershirt and trousers, then pushes the chair back. The heat is palpable, a thick garment wrapping his skin.

He sees the kill jar on the shelf and remembers. The spider. He picks up the jar, wipes the dust off it.

The snow has long since melted and evaporated. At the bottom of the jar lies a desiccated black speck. Byrne shakes it out onto the palm of his hand. Under the magnifying glass he counts the eyes, notes the mottled colouration on the thorax.

The spider's legs uncurl and it scuttles across Byrne's palm. He flicks it back into the jar, opens the door of the hut and steps out onto bare rock. The lunar cold stuns him.

Space blooms with stars.

He crouches, lowers the jar to the snow and

shakes it. The spider drops out and crawls slowly away over the shadowed, granular snow. Byrne stands up and looks out into the darkness.

The distant lights of the icefield chalet are the only signs of human presence. He can see the lamps along the promenade that give it the look of an ocean liner. The tall windows filled with light.

To study accurately the variations in temperature and flow rate, it was necessary to live on the glacier for several consecutive days.

When the temperature drops at dusk to below zero, all the streams on the glacier surface cease to flow. Everywhere the ice bristles up with glittering frost needles as the melted and now refreezing surface water dilatates. A garden of tiny ice flowers seems to be growing all around me.

17

Elspeth walks along the chalet promenade and sees the wink of Byrne's lamp across the valley. She imagines herself an astronomer, and the distant light a constellation of a single star: The Doctor.

18

Glacial ice is not a liquid, nor is it a solid. It flows like lava, like melting wax, like honey. Supple glass. Fluid stone.

To watch it flow, one must be patient. There are few changes that can be seen in the course of one day. But over time crevasses split open and others close. There are ice quakes that shift the terrain, unpredictable geysers of meltwater that carry away ice aiguilles and other land-marks. And of course the evidence of flow, acts of delicate, random precision: shards of rock are plucked by the ice from their strata, carried miles downstream, and left lying with fragments from another geological age.

19

He asks Lightning Bolt, the old man in the telegraph office, for messages from home.

—If there were any, Lightning Bolt mutters, glancing up over his pince-nez, you'd already have them.

There are days when Byrne sinks into a dull lethargy. At these times he goes to the hot spring pool.

He arrives there one morning out of the rain, shivering and pale.

—You're not sitting out there like this, Elspeth says.

Elspeth takes him inside, sits him down on a chair in the warm kitchen and brings in towels, a basin of hot water.

—This has happened to me at least once a year since the accident, he tells her. It's like a recurrence of the hypothermia.

—It's no wonder, she says. You tramp around in the mank all day.

—In the what?

—The mank. The wet. She shakes her head, tugs at his soaked shirtsleeve. This.

—It's a good word, he says. It sounds right.

—I'm surprised you've never heard it before.

He looks down at her hand, which she has kept on his sleeve, and then up into her quietly laughing eyes.

—And this is a hand, she says. You've got two.

—I . . . yes.

He nods and laughs, a short huff of breath. She hands him one of the towels.

—Thank you.

She sets the basin down at his feet and leaves the room.

20

During the next week he travels up and down the line, busy with a routine inspection of camp conditions. He suspects cholera in two men and accompanies them to Edmonton on the train. Late one evening he returns to the chalet without seeing Elspeth, and the next morning he is back on the ice with his notebook.

Seracs. Massive, unstable pinnacles of ice often form in the icefall.

Here, as the glacier flows over a steep grade in the bedrock, internal stresses split and tear the ice. It buckles and heaves into a tortuous topography.

Byrne watches for three days as an architectural wonder is created. The glacier groans, cracks, thunders, and rears up a cathedral.

On the nunatak Byrne lies on his stomach and sketches in his notebook.

When the sun breaks through cloud, the cathedral fills with light. The warmer air hollows it into a more baroque, flamboyant shape. Spires, archways, gargoyles begin to flow. Waterfalls set festive ice bells ringing.

Then, slowly, the delicate balance that kept it aloft is undermined. Even as light glorifies it, the cathedral is diminished, begins almost imperceptibly to collapse. Sepulchral booms and crashes attest to hidden vaults and hollows, the shifting instability of the foundation.

No one can predict exactly when a serac will

give way and topple back into the landscape. The next morning Byrne climbs to the icefall's base to find that the cathedral is gone, swallowed up in its demesne.

Vanished, he writes in his notebook. *It must have fallen quickly, in the night. But it made no sound.*

He realizes it has been almost two weeks since he last saw her. Twelve days of the brief alpine summer. In another month he will be returning to England. He remembers the touch of her hand on his arm.

In the afternoon he hikes back down to the chalet. He is told by the desk clerk that she has been in Jasper for the past three days.

He takes the train into town.

She is here somewhere, perhaps at the general store, or visiting friends. Searching for her, he begins on the outer streets, flanked by the railroad track on one side of the long, narrow town, and the dark bulk of Bear Hill on the other. He makes the brief circuit of Jasper three times, moving inward, stopping in to talk with Trask's son Jim at his father's gift shop, watching the doorway to see if she will stroll past. He halts at last in front of Father Buckler's unfinished stone church. The sun has almost set and its dusty golden light stretches into the valley from the corridor of the Miette River. The lamps are coming on along the street.

He continues his orbit of Jasper, moving outward again, a cold satellite glowing with secret fire.

She is here somewhere. He will meet her soon. She will look into his eyes and realize that he has finally seen her.

21

He checks his pocketwatch and realizes that the last train for the chalet will be leaving soon. If he misses it, he will be stuck in town for the night.

Hurrying back to the main street he catches sight of her, on the steps of the sloping lawn that fronts the warden's office. She is with an old couple, two small, frail-looking people. The old man has long, silky white hair that gleams like an unkempt halo in the lamplight.

Elspeth is pointing across the river, towards Signal Mountain, its peak caught in the fleeting amber of sunset. Standing close to her, the old man and woman listen to what she is saying and nod their heads. Byrne thinks of two seagulls, battered and dazed as if they had just flown through a storm, and now huddled under the shelter of a loving wing. The scene might be one for a sentimental painting, Byrne thinks. *Evening in Jasper.*

Her parents. He recalls that recently she had

talked of them. She was hoping they might visit her. At that time, he had envisioned two tall, stern figures, disapproving in principle of the place their daughter had come to live, sourly listing off the inconveniences of the voyage the moment they stepped from the train. Plain, dour, undemonstrative folk.

And now he sees them laughing at something she has said, her father's hand in hers, her mother gazing up at her. A look of wonder at a daughter grown so tall and graceful and strong.

He hesitates. The bell on the station platform clangs. Elspeth glances across the street and sees him. She waves. Byrne nods and then turns abruptly, hurrying down the stone steps into the station.

22

As the chalet train pulls out of the station, someone taps him on the shoulder. He turns. Elspeth. He gets up and slides into the seat beside her.

—When I saw you, he says, I thought you were staying in town. I'm sorry. . . . I didn't want to miss the train.

—We were just saying goodbye. My parents are taking the eastbound in the morning.

She brushes back a stray lock of hair, a nervous gesture he has never seen before. He realizes she has been struggling to keep back tears. For a moment he thinks his behaviour on the street is to blame, and then remembers the leave-taking she has just come from. Unlike him, she stays in Jasper every winter. It may be years before she sees her family again.

—You didn't have to worry about the train, she says. They wouldn't dare leave without me.

23

Byrne takes Elspeth up to the glacier. Snow has fallen for two days, dusting the lower glacier and even piling into drifts higher up, near the nunatak. They climb the lateral moraine to avoid crevasses and then strike out over the snow, roped together, Byrne hacking with his ice axe every few steps.

They come to an open space of level ice that Byrne cleared of snow the day before.

Byrne walks out carefully onto the bare ice surface, testing its strength after a morning of warm sun. He reaches a spot where a thin sheet of meltwater has accumulated on the ice. He steadies himself with the ice axe and leans his weight on one foot. The ice gives slightly, and he hears the chirrup of air bubbles rising into the water. He steps back. A hairline crack has formed in the ice under his boot. He turns and treads carefully back to the snowbank. Elspeth has disap-

peared. Her boot prints lead up the side of the snow
dune.

—Elspeth?

—Over here. . . .

Her voice is muffled by snow and wind, so that
he can only make out a few words.

—Snow angel. . . .

Byrne drops one of his skates.

—What?

He sees her hand waving from behind the
wind-chiseled crest of the dune, and climbs to her. She
smiles, gestures to the winged impression she has created in the deeper, drifted snow of the hollow.

—I haven't made one of these since I was a little
girl. I'd forgotten how lovely they are.

He crouches beside her.

—Your turn, she says, her smile fading at his
intense, misplaced gaze. He is looking past her at the
shape her body has left in the snow.

—It's beautiful.

She flicks up a gloveful of snow that powders
into his face.

—Oh. She puts a hand over her mouth. I didn't
mean for that to happen.

He smiles, wipes at his eyes with his scarf.

—It feels. . . .

—Tell me.

—Like this.

He sinks beside her onto the snow. With her lips she brushes away the snow on his eyelids, his forehead. He bends to her. They touch each other with their faces, their wrists, the only skin left bare in the cold.

—Are we going to skate?

—I don't think so.

24

—I like that, he says.

—What?

—The way you touch the page with your fingers as you read.

She puts down the paper cover copy of *Wuthering Heights*. She is sitting up on the bed, a blanket over her bare shoulders. He lies beside her. The latched door of the shelter rattles in the wind.

—I suppose I like the change in texture, when you pass from the type to the margin. The feel of the blank page around the words.

His mouth creases in amusement.

—You can feel that?

—Well, I imagine I can. Sometimes I think it's half the pleasure of reading.

He props himself up on one elbow.

—There's something I want you to see. Some of my notes.

—No. No more history. No more dates and little-known facts.

He slides from the bed, across to his worktable, and thumbs through his stack of notebooks.

—If you want to know what I'm really doing out here every day. . . .

—I think I do.

—Then read this.

—I'd rather hear it from you.

—It wouldn't come out right. I would simplify things too much. This will give you the uncertainty.

She takes the book he has opened, his finger pointing out the place where she should begin. These are the notes he made after his trip to Paris, when he shut himself up in his London flat, pacing, gazing out the window. Elspeth reads and he remembers the writing.

25

First the crevasse. Everything he could remember. The winged shape. And then notes from memory of the stories told him by Sara, by the settler Swift on the journey to Edmonton.

Notes that lead nowhere, that circle back on themselves. Notes taken while studying Sexsmith's memoir of his travels in the Rocky Mountains. Sexsmith's tales of hunting adventures, a bare mention of the Stoney brothers and the young woman. Nothing about the map on her palm, just the observation that she was a sort of *good luck charm* for the brothers. And of the icefield, not one word. Sexsmith wrote of his decision to turn back, blaming it on fatigue and the grumbling of the men.

Notes that Byrne took as he read everything he could find on glaciers and the ice ages. The romantic Agassiz, John Tyndall the cool-headed Victorian, the methodical observations of the Vaux family.

He copied out Tyndall's quiet confessions:

I was soon upon the ice, once more alone, as I delight to be at times.

For Tyndall, a greater mystery than glacial dynamics was the human imagination. From *a few scattered observations* it had dared to reconstruct the prehistory of the world. Was imagination, he wondered, an energy *locked like latent heat in ancient inorganic nature?*

Or rather, Byrne wrote in his journal, *was it a power that overflowed from some unseen source, pressing inexorably forward to enclose and reshape the world?*

And with that thought, a fact he had always known and yet ignored rose into the light of significance. Glaciers are rivers. Water.

He stood up, went over to the window of his study and opened it. The sky was a white roof from which rain dropped like melting snow. Leaning on the sill in his shirtsleeves, he gazed down the wet ravine of the street, breathed in the damp ash odour of London air.

The basic paradox: frozen flow. Fragments embedded in the ice do not move, yet are ceaselessly in motion.

Below him, foot passengers and horses pulling carriages struggled through the slush. In the gutter a troupe of shouting children were building a wall of dirty snow.

As the ice flows downward from its site of accumulation, it descends into a warmer climatic zone and begins to melt. If the amount of summer melt exceeds the rate of advance, the glacier wastes away, recedes. To early European observers in the Alps it seemed that the more swiftly receding glaciers were actually crawling backwards up the mountain. In a single day and night, land previously buried would reappear.

In the Alps, the bodies of missing mountaineers have emerged from the wasting ice of glaciers decades, perhaps even centuries, after they were lost.

He paced around the flat, a glass of sherry balanced on the palm of his hand. The fumes rose to his nostrils, potent, innervating. He sat down and read over what he had just written:

Immense pressure, coupled with extreme cold. Combining to produce hitherto unknown effects on matter. Or upon spirit.

The possibility of a spiritual entity trapped, frozen, in ice. Enmeshed somehow in physical forces, immobilized, and thus rendered physical and solid itself.

He finished the sherry, set the glass down, and turned again to the window. The thin lace curtain billowed with a breath of wind and sank back again.

And when it melted out of the ice, would it then just sublimate back into metaphysical space, leaving human time and scientific measurement behind?

If I could be there, observe it, at the moment of escape.

26

He turns from stoking the last embers of the fire, steps across the frozen floor on tiptoe as though over hot coals. He stands hunched over the bed for a moment, rubs his naked arms and chest, marvels at the brief sparks that light his fingertips.

He smiles. Friction, heat. Did her body pass this blue fire to his? It must be an effect of the dry air, the fine dust that settles imperceptibly, ceaselessly, on everything at this elevation.

He climbs between the cool sheets. She is somewhere beside him in the bed, already asleep, but he cannot feel her warmth. He lies on his stomach, listening for her breathing. At times she moves slightly, a hand, a leg, sliding across the blanket like a whisper. A word spoken in a dream.

They are swimming side by side in a night lake, their bodies never touching. Only the waves of breathing tell of the other's presence.

She had said to him, when she finished the pages he asked her to read, *So you want to know what I think?*

He was standing by the fireplace, arms crossed over his chest.

—You don't have to tell me, he said.

—You won't like it.

—Tell me.

She set the notebook on the bed beside her.

—I don't know what this thing was, is, will turn out to be, and right now it doesn't seem to matter.

—I see.

—You should read my journal. Pages of *what is he thinking? Can he tell what I'm feeling? Would he care?*

—This, she waved a hand at the notebook, the fact that you let me read this, it's my first bit of tangible evidence. I ought to rush home this instant and write it down. Day forty-nine: a breakthrough. I believe the creature now trusts me.

—That's funny, he said.

—Then laugh.

He sat down beside her on the bed.

—To be honest, she said, I don't think you saw anything in the crevasse.

—You mean I imagined it.

—I mean you saw something, but my guess is, as you said yourself, it might have been a natural shape formed by the ice. Only I would add, not might have been, but probably was.

—You would have made a good scientist. I didn't know you were so unromantic.

—Am I? When I was a girl I believed in the fairies, even though I'd never seen one. I was told it was all foolishness and superstition, but of course I didn't care. One day I went with my brother up the hill above our town, to find a pony that had strayed. But I couldn't keep up with Sandy. As usual, he was in a hurry. I was a nuisance, he said, he had to keep stopping and waiting for me, and finally he told me to turn around and go home. I sulked and wandered for a while, and then I sat down by a stream. On the other side was a great wild hawthorn, and I let out a shriek when I saw there was a girl standing there, in the shade of the leaves. I jumped up. I said hello and waved my hand. She just stood there on the other side of that stream and watched me. Her eyes were green. She was elfin, beautiful. I felt that this was her place on the earth, her life had grown here and was rooted here like the hawthorn, and I was an intruder. I ran home, frightened out of my scarce enough wits, but almost every day after that I would climb the hill, hoping I'd see her again.

—But you never did.

—Freya reminds me of her, but no, I never did.

—And you've always wanted to know whether she was a dream, a vision, or just an ordinary girl under a tree.

—Yes, but she was not ordinary. That's just it. Years later I thought, she didn't have to be a spirit, a fairy, anything like that. She didn't have to be from another world, to fill mine with magic. I'd never seen anyone, anything, like her. A beautiful girl under a hawthorn, that's enough of a wonder, isn't it?

27

—I wanted to introduce you to my parents.

—As what?

—My friend the doctor. They only saw you from a distance, and you managed to keep it that way.

—Tell me something about your father.

—Oh, he's a fierce man. When my brother and I would fight, he had a truly horrible punishment for us.

—What was it?

—He made us hold hands and sing.

28

—Thank you, she says.

—For what?

—For bringing me here, where no one can find me. I haven't had peace and quiet like this for months. Even on my days off they come looking for me with some problem.

—They won't come looking for you up here.

—No, I don't think they will.

—This will be your chalet. You're the guest whose every whim will be indulged. And you can stay as long as you like.

—No, I can't.

29

—And what did you think?

—About what?

—When you got better, and your mother said it was a miracle. Did you believe that too?

—I don't know.

—You don't remember?

—I remember too much.

—But not that.

—I just mean I didn't know if it was a miracle, and I still don't. But because my mother believed it,

I wanted to believe it too. I became very religious. I even thought about the priesthood. I wanted to be like Saint Francis of Assisi, living in the wilderness, loving every living thing, even the trees and the rocks, everything. Then one day, about four years after my father and I moved to London, I was in church by myself, and I got up and walked out and that was the end of it. Just like that. Later that year I told my father I wanted to be a doctor.

—How old were you?

—Fourteen or fifteen. I just dropped it, the great passion of my life, and walked away.

—And what about this great passion, the ice?

—There are times I hate this place. But I keep coming back, as if I'm condemned to do this.

Once this world had been on the periphery of his imagination, a place from which one returned to tell the tale. Now it has become the centre of his field of vision. And more than central: inevitable. From this vantage point, for good or ill, he believes that his life could have taken no other road.

The contours of the icefield, even those he cannot see and must envision from the maps of others, now seem to embody a form he has sensed vaguely all his life.

Trask nudges Hal with an elbow.

—I don't believe it. Look.

Hal follows his pointing finger past the corral fence, down the sloping lawn to the footpath where Elspeth and Byrne are climbing into view.

Trask shakes his head.

—I cannot for the life of me understand what she sees in him. The man's spent so much time on that glacier I'll bet he shoots icicles.

31

The next day Elspeth returns, unexpected, to visit him. Freya is with her, but she says very little, inspects the shelter and then stands in the doorway, looking out at the glacier.

—A bachelor's hideout, she says. Nothing new.

—You shouldn't have come up on your own, Byrne says.

—She didn't, Freya says. I'm here.

Elspeth sets a basket on his worktable.

—There's some cold roast beef, potatoes, rolls. And an orange.

They smile at each other, at their shyness in the presence of Freya.

—Wonderful, Byrne says. Especially the orange. Scurvy is a hazard of this kind of work.

—So is insanity, Freya says.

She tugs a small book out of her jacket pocket and holds it out to Byrne.

—I brought you something too, she says.

He takes the book and opens it to the title page. A tattered volume of plays by Shakespeare.

—I found it by the outlet of Grizzly Creek, in an old circle of campfire stones. Elspeth told me you collected things like this.

The pages of the leatherbound book are swollen from years of exposure to wind and rain. A dry deposit of grit in the gutter. The print has faded, but in many places miniscule marginal notes can be seen.

He examines the book from front cover to back. Stamped on the endpaper is a heraldic family crest: on a field of azure, a celestial city, proper. And the motto: *J'espère.* Freya leans forward.

—Do you know who lost it?

—Yes.

32

This book may have been mislaid by Sexsmith, Byrne writes in his notebook that evening, *or he may have left it with Viraj. And then perhaps it was tossed aside by the* surveyors after they had plundered and torn down the trading post.

Almost all of the marginal notes concern the plays. But in the last pages are a few scratchy lines about the icefield. And a hastily scribbled map with a blank area at its centre. Byrne copies everything into his own journal. He pieces together the final hours of Sexsmith's quest.

33

Before them lies a sea of drifting, hissing snow. On all sides indistinct peaks rise like islands above the blurred horizon. Sunlight gleams fitfully on the ice cap of the highest summit, far across the plain from where they stand.

They take shelter in the lee of a rock outcrop at the edge of the open expanse. The Stoney brothers build a thrifty fire with scraps of wood saved from the last encampment.

Sexsmith says nothing. He stares out at the white expanse, watches it disappear slowly behind a wall of blowing snow. While the brothers cook a meal, Sexsmith goes for a walk onto the snow field in the fading light of dusk. The relentless wind soon turns him back. It is obvious that no animals come here to graze. There is nothing to hunt, there will be no way to replenish the food supply.

All that I see is stale, flat, unprofitable.

He has left his journal with Viraj. The only book he carries with him now contains the Bard's least inspiring creations. *Antony and Cleopatra. A Midsummer Night's Dream.* Back at the camp, in his tent, he lights the lamp and tries to read, but his wind-blistered eyes are too sore. Instead he makes a few perfunctory marginal notes, pushing the pen with numb, blistered fingers to form words he can barely see.

In the raw morning, Sexsmith sips his tea while the Stoney brothers pack up the camp.

Sexsmith spills a few drops of tea onto the snow at his feet. They disappear instantly, even the brown stain absorbed into the white surface.

He digs absently with the toe of his boot. There is a faint blue shadow in the hollow where the spilled liquid fell. He crouches, brushes away the snow crust with his gloved hands, digging a hole into the powdery layers beneath. Further down the snow solidifies again. Sexsmith stabs his alpenstock into the hole, strikes a hard surface. Rock, he thinks, and scrapes at it, glimpses a faint reflected gleam.

Blue, silver. What is it?

He pours the remains of his tea into the hole, hacks at it with the point of the alpenstock. Crystalline shards fly out.

Ice.

He understands now that he is walking across a

bowl of ice on the top of the world. The glaciers have been spilling from its brim.

Nothing. A dreary waste of ice.

The brothers have shouldered their packs and stand waiting for Sexsmith. He turns away and stalks out into the icefield, hacking at the snow crust with his alpenstock. The brothers follow. Sexsmith stumbles in the deepening snow and halts as the brothers approach. He hears them and turns, a bitter smile on his face.

A spirit place.

That evening they make it to the camp on the ridge. In his journal, the pages blotched with frozen tears from his inflamed eyes, Sexsmith writes nothing about the plain of ice. Only the date and

Disappointment.

34

But was that all? Byrne wonders. Why would he keep silent about it? Unless, like me, he encountered something that he dared not set down in his memoirs.

Disappointment. Nothing but snow, ice, cloud, wind. That was all he found. And what he could not accept. A world with a wasteland like this at its summit.

After many notebook pages of measurement and calculation, Byrne writes down a year, places a question mark beside it. *In the summer of that year,* he writes, *the region of the glacier into which I fell should reach the terminus. Rather, it will be the terminus, and will therefore begin to melt.*

Whatever is embedded within it must, by the laws of nature, reappear.

❄

Hal

*She is somehow childlike. This older woman who has
lived in some of the world's great cities and written
about their dangers, their seductions. She travels like
the meandering heroine of a novel for children, shrug-
ging off the entanglements of one chapter and moving
on to the next, never stopping long enough in one place
for its habits of defeat and cynicism to cling to her.
Always asking* what's over the next hill, around the
next curve of the river? *But never asking* how will
I get home?

*For me, every new encounter is a confrontation
from which I withdraw into solitude, to examine myself
for the marks of deformation. The world is forever
pounding on my character, such as it is, shaping it the
way water patiently shapes a rock.*

Freya is a waterfall.

*This winter I've been reading some of her maga-
zine pieces. I find it almost impossible to read them with*

any kind of objectivity. The fact is, I find it almost impossible to read them at all. I suppose I'm looking for Freya in her writing, and she's not there.

I've learned a lot, though, about her working method. The way she impinges on a world and then records its shifts and adjustments to her presence. This is not arrogance or willful blindness on her part. I see that now. She once told me that only in this way can she remain truthful to the people and the cultures she encounters. She can't pretend to be an invisible translator of another way of life, a recording angel hovering somewhere above the scene. Touching the skin of an unfamiliar city, she knows she has become part of what she touches, but she may never know exactly how. Her trace is quickly lost. If she places herself in the foreground of her narratives it is because she knows this, that her words can only be a transcription of an elusive, endlessly recurring moment of first contact.

In her swift passage through a new world she moves like a bullet. A small violence. Her writing a record of damage. ✴

ABLATION ZONE

The firn line, between the inviolate and the

melting zones of a glacier, is often sharply defined.

Once past this point the ice begins to die.

Melting can be hastened by even a faint increase in

heat at the lower extremity of a glacier, such as

produced by the flash bulbs of hundreds of cameras.

1

In June of the following summer the alpine club gathers at Arcturus creek. In keeping with tradition, everyone gathers around a bonfire on the first evening to tell stories and make plans for the days ahead.

When the fire has died to pale embers, Freya hears someone approach from the dark beyond the circle of light.

—Fine evening.

The stranger stands back in the shadows thrown by the others gathered there, and Freya cannot see his face. The flare of a match appears for a moment, a hand cupped around the bowl of a pipe, the glint of an eye, a sharp cheekbone.

They are discussing the quality of the rock in the region.

—It's true, the stranger says. The rock is not the best for climbing.

And he goes on in detail about the composition of several rock faces, the various grades of limestone and quartz. Freya follows his words for some time, but then, lulled by the fire's warmth, she no longer hears the words but listens only to the sound of the voice. After a while she feels she is floating in space, buoyed up on the rising and falling of the stranger's voice.

She can hear, rolling underneath the cold technical language, a turbulence of desires and emotions. She cannot interpret them. This is a voice out of the dark.

Then the stranger stops talking. He bids everyone a good night. The swish of his long raincoat, his footfalls, recede into the cold dark beyond the circle of bodies. Freya turns to Hal.

—That was Doctor Byrne, she says, realizing it even as she speaks his name.

When the fire has gone dark, violet bands of aurora borealis appear in the night sky. Freya and Hal watch them shimmer, fade and reappear. Freya remembers a story she was told as a child.

—The aurora was the radiance of a beautiful ice maiden. She lived far in the north, and her coldness repelled all suitors. But the king of elves and flowers fell in love with her, and his desire melted her frozen heart. That is how spring came.

Hal glances at her while she speaks. Her face, her words: he feels there must be a clue there for him about what he might say. She's told him a love story, but he already knows she has moved away from him.

He sensed it already last summer. And he knew it when she appeared at the stable the evening of her arrival. She hadn't sent a message asking him to meet her at the station. Her greeting, lips grazing his forehead, was the message. Hello, love, goodbye.

Perhaps this summer she will have enough material gathered for a book about Jasper. He wonders if he will be excised from it, like the thief over the side of the houseboat.

And tonight all she wants to talk about is their upcoming climb together. *Together,* he thinks.

And Byrne. She is intrigued by him.

—He's a useful source of information. He knows the ice, at any rate. It wouldn't hurt to have a longer chat with him.

Rawson laughs.

—A *chat* with him, Freya? He doesn't chat, he drones. And besides, he has to be aware of your existence first.

—So I'll seduce him and then we'll chat.

—That unfortunate man.

3

Freya visits Byrne at his shelter. She decided not to wait for Rawson, but to go see him herself before anyone else thought of the idea. She got a fire going well before dawn, drank some coffee and then set out, passing between the neat rows of white canvas tents and into the till plain, arriving at the nunatak as the sun rose over Arcturus peak.

—If you go up the glacier, stick to the south moraine, Byrne tells her. He showed little surprise at her unexpected knock on the shelter door, and even less pleasure.

—There's not so much melting and crevasse activity in the mountain's shadow.

—What about the icefield itself? she asks. To her surprise he looks vaguely embarrassed, uncomfortable. He runs a finger along the spine of a book on his table.

—I haven't been up that far. I've never seen the icefield. Since the crevasse accident I can't climb steep gradients. My arm gives out. So I'm limited to the lower reaches.

She looks at him, wide-eyed.

—That's ridiculous. You can come with us. Three would be more to Trask's liking anyway. And it would ease some of Hal's worries. We'll help you on the difficult pitches.

He shakes his head.

—I'm really no climber. I would endanger the two of you.

She argues. He is a sheer wall. She does not like to yield, but his refusal is final. She shakes her head in frustration.

—So what can you know about the icefield if you've never been up there? Nothing.

He smiles.

—I've learned a lot from the glacier itself. A way of looking at the rest of the world. Patience. Control of the emotions.

—That's wonderful, if you happen to be ice.

She shakes her head, concedes defeat, asks to take his photograph. He agrees, realizing that this will be the first time he has been captured on film since he first left England on the expedition.

They step outside for the light. After she takes the picture, she taps her camera and says,

—This will bring back your icefield.

He asks her to take note of anything unusual, and to let him know about it when she returns.

—How do you define unusual? she asks, studying him.

He meets her inquiring gaze and glances away, leans forward to sort the papers scattered over the table.

—Anything unexpected, he says.

Her breath in his ear. He looks up, shocked, into her eyes.

—You mean something like that.

4

Freya and Hal plot the climb of Mount Meru, considering routes on maps and on the diorama in the chalet lobby that Trask has had constructed. A three-dimensional model with tiny scale replicas of the chalet and outbuildings, and the surrounding peaks, all under clear glass. The inconveniently vast icefield is truncated by the edge of the display.

—I know Meru has been climbed before, Freya tells Hal. But I want to try it, for myself. It'll also give me the chance to cross part of the icefield. Just so I can say I've done it.

Rawson has climbed before, but not on ice. They practise belays, cutting ice steps, glissades. And at Byrne's suggestion the next time he meets with Freya, crevasse rescue.

They do their best to avoid Trask. He would recommend a team approach, six or seven climbers, the way that Freya reached the summits of Arcturus and Parnassus. Even though this will not be a first ascent, nor an especially difficult one, he would frown upon Freya's choice of Hal, who is not an official climbing guide. In no time Trask would take over the entire expedition.

—Trask and I share an ancient animosity, Freya says. City builder and nomad. I raid his town, ignore his restrictions and guard rails, and he tells scandalous stories about me.

—You don't care? Hal asks.

—I've stopped caring. I realized that the more I goad people like him, the better the material I get. Breaking rules gives me my best copy.

They hike to the mountain's base every day, and climb adjacent hills to get a better view. Through his field glasses, Hal picks out an unusual pattern on a snow slope of Meru. A series of vertical lines, blue-shadowed seams in the snow.

—Those lines are larger than they look from here, Freya says. More like vertical hillocks when you're traversing them, which I personally like to avoid. In the Himalayas some of the climbers call that effect Parvati's Curtain.

—Is there somewhere on this planet you haven't been?

—Lots of places. Up there, for one.

They set up their base camp at the foot of Arcturus glacier, which they will ascend on the first day of the climb. From there they will traverse across part of the icefield, to reach the less precipitous slope of Meru.

5

—What do you think of Byrne? she asks.

They are walking up the glacier from the doctor's shelter.

—I admire some of his qualities—his coolheadedness, his keen eye. He's forged himself an impressive suit of armour. But I can't really relax in his presence. I don't know how anyone could. He doesn't let that facade crack, not that I've ever seen.

—He does. With Elspeth.

—What's this about?

—I'm wondering what keeps him coming out here day after day. He's looking for something, or waiting for something. What is it? And the icefield. It's like some kind of sacred place to him. I mean, it's got a certain fascination, I can understand that, but for him it's something more. He can't wait for us to come back and give him a full report.

—We could make up stories, when we get back, about what we found up there. The ruins of a lost civilization or something. And see how he reacts.

—No, I couldn't do that. This place is the man's obsession.

She walks on ahead.

6

An overhanging carapace of ice, hollowed underneath by melting, forms a dome illuminated from above by the sun. Freya hacks steps to it, and Hal follows.

They stand together, watching as capillaries of water run and swirl along the translucent ceiling of the dome. In places the thin trails flow together, swirl and let fall a spray of glittering droplets. They can see a whole labyrinthine network of interlacing rivulets, lit by the sun, threading among the rounded crystals of the deliquescing ice. Freya sets up her camera and squints into the viewfinder, then turns to Hal.

—I sometimes have the feeling the ice is alive.

7

They cross the bergschrund to the north face and step onto a steep slope of icy limestone. From here it will be a short vertical pitch to the icefield.

Midway up the rock face they discover a niche, a place to huddle and rest for a moment. They edge toward it. A knife wind off the ice above whips glittering shards into their eyes. Hal stumbles into the niche, blinded. He slips on a seam of verglas, slams his knee painfully against the rock.

Freya kneels beside him, clutches his arm. For a moment, in the haze of snow, she is a stranger.

He thinks, *What am I doing here with this person?*

For an exhilarating moment he can't think of anything that he knows about her. There is no history and no impending future without her. He leans forward to touch her face and she moves away, her hand slipping down his arm to grip his hand and help him to his feet. He remembers.

8

With field glasses Byrne keeps watch on Meru. He knows the two climbers will not be visible until they reach the peak. He hopes then to catch a glimpse of them. Freya agreed she would flash a mirror from the summit.

The sliver of icefield he can see from the nunatak is painfully bright in the morning sun. The edge of a radiant white planet rising too close to the earth. He lowers the field glasses and rubs his eyes.

He ducks back into the shelter, the red branch of an afterimage floating before him in the dark. He sits down at the table where he has been working.

Trask has asked him to put together a short primer on ice and glaciers, to accompany his diorama with its interestingly misspelled inscription:

Ariel View of Jasper and Environs

He sets aside an earlier draft and picks up his pen, begins again on a fresh sheet of paper.

The icefield is the source of several major river systems, and a storehouse of fresh water. The layers of ice deep within the field may be hundreds of years old, formed from snow that fell here before the discovery of America, before the birth of Shakespeare, before the industrial revolution.

He writes of the Swiss glaciologist Louis Agassiz, and quotes his dramatic imagining of the *Eiszeit*, the great ice age of the past:

The land we call Europe,
before that time a tropical jungle
inhabited by elephants, enormous
reptiles and gigantic tigers, was
swiftly buried beneath a great
sheet of ice covering valleys,
plateaus, and mountains. Over all
descended the silence of death. The
rays of the sun, shining down on a
frozen world, were met only by the
shriek of the wind, and the groan-
ing of crevasses as they yawned
open across the surface of this vast
ocean of ice.

Agassiz was also the first scientist to speculate
that ice ages and subsequent warming periods have
recurred many times in geological history. He eventually
came to believe that each glacial epoch obliterated all life
on earth, and that when the ice receded an entirely new
creation arose. He felt this would explain the many mys-
terious gaps in the fossil record.

While the idea of the utter extinction and regener-
ation of life has long been discredited, there is no doubt
that the global climate has fluctuated greatly in the past,
and that the ages of ice have greatly affected all living
things, including the human race.

Some scientists believe, in fact, that it is to the effects of the most recent ice age we owe the emergence of early civilization.

The onset of this glacial epoch, hundreds of thousands of years ago, must have brought catastrophic change to the earth's surface. Previously lush vegetation dwindled. Many animal species vanished, evolved, or migrated. The early tribes of humans, once simple hunters and gatherers, were forced into a nomadic existence, into the unknown, and they needed new tools for the journey. New ways of thinking. New words.

Byrne sets down his pen. Stories. They took their stories with them, to remind them who they were. And there were the tales brought back by those who scouted ahead. They moved through stories.

Byrne sits back in his chair. This isn't what he was asked to write. Trask wants his tourists to have the model, a brief explanatory text, and a view of the real thing. Prehistory will come alive for them, they will commemorate the moment by buying postcards, souvenirs, film for photographs.

In his enthusiasm for the idea Trask also considered a dome of blue, rather than transparent, glass. To illustrate fancifully how the site where the town lies was once submerged under ice. He then decided that would be too frightening, and might possibly offend the religious.

9

Byrne copies the words of Agassiz into his journal.

"No one can say exactly what physical forces are responsible for the recurring ages of ice. Nor is it known how long we have before our own, perhaps brief, summer comes to an end."

10

They halt for the night at the edge of the icefield, pitching camp in the lee of a rock buttress. In the wedge tent, lit by a hanging lantern, they suck pastilles to soothe their burning throats. Hal brews coffee on the portable camp stove, mixes it with a few drops of rum in aluminum cups.

Fists of wind hammer the tent walls.

They are alone together. Out on the mountain they were kept distanced by the rigours and discipline of climbing. Now they are inches away from each other in this tiny tent. They make halting conversation about the wind, the cold, the next day's climb. Freya builds a wall of talk about the difficulty of photography in such vast natural landscapes. A vista that is breathtaking to the eye rarely keeps that awe-inspiring grandeur intact on film.

—You have to know what to leave out. You have to choose some detail to . . . suggest all the rest of it.

They are tired and the subject is soon exhausted. Freya inspects her camera, cleans the lenses.

Rawson sits uneasily under the swinging light that seems a moving figure of their unspoken thought, crossing the silence between them. He props his journal on his knees, reads over what he has written. Notes for a poem about ice:

Colors: blue, gray, white
Arts: architecture, sculpture, music
Hour: crepuscular
Senses: vision, touch
Organs: skin, lungs, skeleton
Artifacts: glass, porcelain, bone, paper
Contraries: blood, passion, Freya
Planets: Mercury, Pluto
Glaciers are seraphic. Think of Antarctica, embraced by a vast angel of ice.

—The wind really wants in, she says.

He looks up over his journal at her. She is digging in her rucksack, not looking at him.

Freya takes out a porcelain pipe, a smoking kit from a small tin case. She fills the pipe, lights it, and leans back against her piled gear to smoke.

—The look on your face, she laughs, handing

the pipe to him. As he takes it she says with mock solemnity,

—I should warn you, that's not any ordinary fine cut.

He sniffs at the sweetly pungent smoke curling out of the pipe.

—This is what? Hashish?

She nods.

—I first tried it in Darjeeling. Wonderful for fatigue, depression, nervous strain.

He allows himself an acid smile.

—Well then, hand it over. It's just what the doctor ordered.

—What's that supposed to mean?

—Nothing. Only I think the air's a bit thin up here for the intoxicating perfumes of the East.

She shakes her head.

—I thought you poets were supposed to thrive on new sensations.

He leans forward and takes the pipe. Again he is the novice. With her, his only role. He takes a drag on the pipe, the acrid smoke searing his throat. Tensing himself against the urge to cough, he glares defiantly over her head, his eyes welling with tears.

He leans back and puffs out a perfect, redeeming smoke ring.

—Don't puff it, Freya says, poking a finger through the collapsing ring. Drink it. Savour it.

—Anything for you, my love.

—Hal. . . .

He sucks in another mouthful of smoke, then hands the pipe back to her. He swallows the smoke, feels it burn into his lungs. He breathes out and his head reels, but in a moment the sensation fades and is gone. His mind and body remain as they were, every ache and blister in place. His gaze focuses again on Freya. She has set the pipe down and is massaging her bare feet.

—Which father am I?

Her eyes flick up at him, glittering.

—Don't. That has nothing to do with us.

—It doesn't? I'm sure I must remind you of one of them. The paper father. The warm milk father. How about the toast and tea father?

—Don't mock that, please, Hal.

—I only want to know which one you're leaving behind this time. So I can try to be one of the others, or even myself, if that's possible. Just tell me how to do it.

She sets the pipe down carefully, her hand trembling, though it may be the wavering light that plays this trick.

Her hand. All her power over him seems concentrated there at this moment. He watches her hand with a sense of desperate urgency.

He thinks, *this is the absolute wrong place for*

this. There's no room in this tent for thunderbolts.

—It wouldn't matter what you did, she says at last. It's me. I don't like hurting you, but I also know I'm not coming back. I never have before. This is how I live.

—Then I'll go with you.

—No.

—I'll follow you. You can't stop me from doing that.

She looks at him with a distant smile.

—Then I guess I'd have to shoot you.

11

They start across the icefield before dawn, carrying candle lanterns. Low cloud banks become visible after an hour. The greater expanse of the field is shrouded from them.

The sky grows steadily lighter and then darkens again suddenly. The wind strengthens. Needle droplets of rain sting their faces.

He hears a note. An unwavering high-pitched hum in the air near him. His ice-axe. He can feel the vibration through his wool gloves. He holds the axe up to examine it.

Freya grabs it out of his hand, flings it away onto the snow.

The electrified air crackles. Green lightning pops overhead and they crouch together as thunder smacks the field. The roar is a long time in dying.

—The enchanted axe, Hal shouts. Sings to warn you. Freya shrugs her shoulders, points to her ear.

Swiftly the storm cloud tumbles overhead, then breaks against the mountain wall.

The sun appears through the thinning veil of cloud, a pale disc. For a moment Hal thinks it must be the moon.

They help each other to their feet. Their hands grip each other's shoulders for a long moment.

Freya breaks the clasp.

—Sorry. All the bells were ringing.

12

He imagines that days are passing as they cross the icefield. There are no reliable landmarks in this sea of snow. They walk in single file, Freya taking the lead. The white expanse opens out as they move forward, growing in immensity the further they penetrate into it. Hummocks that appeared to be quite close recede into distant uplands, vanish completely, or turn, by some trick of light, into hollows down which they stumble, floundering into chest-high snowdrifts.

The world is drained of depth and colour, and he finds himself filling the empty space with phantom figures that silently watch him pass or trudge along with him. One of them is his father, who walks beside him for a while in silence and then says,

Where is this girl taking you, Hal?

Up a mountain, Dad.

It won't last, but you'll be glad you knew her. Someday you'll look back and be glad.

Light bursts briefly through the cloud cover, so intense it presses down like darkness, a negative of midnight. Hal watches Freya's shape drop below the edge of a swale ahead of him. Soon all he can see is the end of the rope that links him to her. For a moment he wonders who is really there at the other end of that swaying line. He stops. The rope pulls taut.

She reappears, reeling in the slack. Breathing hard, he mutters an excuse about the rope getting tangled. She smiles and says something encouraging it seems, but the words are taken by the wind. He is like that now: weightless, soundless, light enough to float up with the whirling ice crystals into the white sky.

I'll be a ghost to her. A lesser shade, haunting some room in her memory she hardly ever enters.

13

A knife-edge ridge of hard, sculpted snow is the last obstacle. Climbing pure geometry. On either side the slope drops away for hundreds of feet into a gloomy cirque.

They dig their ice axes and hobnail boots with greater confidence in this solid surface. They make good time, reaching the summit ridge at twelve-thirty, just as clouds roll in again.

14

They embrace at the summit. A brief, formal clasp.

The space around them is enclosed in ice fog, muffled, like a room. They make a cursory inspection of the cornice, prodding with axe handles for weaknesses, then take turns squinting through the field glasses in an unsuccessful attempt to pick out landmarks. The wind is relentless. They know they cannot stay very long. And suddenly it seems there is very little for them to do here.

—Should we try the mirror, Hal asks, for Byrne?

Freya shakes her head.

—There's no sun.

Biscuits and coffee from a thermos bottle make up a quick summit meal.

While they eat, a gap is torn in the fog. Clouds shred away in the wind. The world is unveiled.

To the southwest stretches the rolling expanse of the icefield. They turn away from its unrelieved whiteness.

Down in the rocky valley the bright red roof of the Hot Springs Chalet. A toy house. Below it, the river's slender curve glitters through trees.

Some nearby peaks they can name by sight: Ammonite, Diadem, Alberta, Stutfield. And closer to them Parnassus, Athabasca, Arcturus. Almost directly below them, hundreds of feet down, stretches the rubble-strewn track of the glacier.

—Can you see Byrne's place?

—I see the nunatak, but I can't make out the shelter. Can you?

—I'm not sure.

Freya begins a contest, to describe the mountains ranged around them. Olympian palaces. The heavenly host bright with all their crowns. Beethoven's Ninth, final movement. Frozen writing desks.

—Damn it, Freya says.

—What?

—I have to pee.

—Not here.

They give in to giddy laughter.

—The mirror, Freya says. They make a hurried search of each other's pack, not sure which of them was carrying it.

Freya shakes her head.

—Forget about it. No time.

She sets up the collapsible tripod and begins snapping pictures with her Panoram portable.

16

She wants to kodak Hal for posterity. He shrugs his assent.

—Stand over there. We'll get the icefield in the background, for Byrne.

—Then I'll take one of you, Hal says. For me.

—Step back, she says, waving a gloved hand. Way back now.

At first he does not understand she is teasing him, so he glances behind to see how far he can safely step. When he turns again to share the joke, she is gone.

In the evening Byrne hears the crunch of footsteps over the snow and sets down his pen. He goes to the door, thinking he will greet both of them and tell them *I'm sorry but I didn't see your signal. I started writing and lost track of time.*

He opens the door. Hal is there, alone. He tries to speak and breaks down. Byrne sits him in the chair and extracts the story.

18

The summit cornice had collapsed.

He crawled to the broken edge and saw only the billowing cloud of snow loosened by her fall.

He retraced their path along the ridge, then crawled away from the trail of their boot prints onto the cliff's sheer face.

He descended methodically, working on each foot and hand hold. Talking to himself about his progress. After some time he realized he was chanting aloud a meaningless litany.

—I am stone, the world is stone, everything is stone.

He found her in a gently sloping snow hollow. She was standing, he saw with a momentary rush of hope, and then thought *this is impossible, she fell three hundred metres.* With that thought he halted, suddenly afraid of her.

She was brushing snow from her wool jacket, and looked vaguely perplexed, like someone who had misplaced her reading glasses.

I'm fine, she said when she was aware of his approach. *Just cold.*

He saw the streak of snow stained red at her feet. She looked past his shoulder as if blind.

Freya. . . .

She turned away, sinking, and he crouched with her, saw the split from temple to ear, the white of bone. She drew her legs up underneath her and settled against him.

He carried her down the slope and onto the glacier. Her head was nestled into the front of his wool jacket. Her body warm and heavy against his. There was so much warmth.

As he staggered down the ice the sun burned the clouds away. The air warmed. He heard the sound of rushing water and followed the winding course of a meltwater stream down-slope to the shore of Byrne's nameless lake. A wide, calm pool, perfectly transparent.

He set her down by the lake and looked into her open, sightless eyes.

20

The two men take rope and blankets back up the glacier to the lake.

They wrap the body and carry it to the shelter, placing it gently on the stone floor. Byrne examines it briefly under the light of his spirit lamp.

—We'll leave her here tonight and return with help tomorrow.

—Leave her?

—Yes, it's too dark now to bring her down.

—You can find the way with your eyes closed, bastard. I'll carry her myself.

—You don't have the strength left. You know that.

Rawson gives in, steps outside.

For the first time, Byrne closes the door of the shelter firmly behind him and blocks it up with several large stones.

21

Elspeth fills a kettle with water and sets it on the stove. She crouches down in front of the wood box, strikes a match, and lights a fire while rocking on her heels. She is not yet fully awake. She watches the paper crumple, the broken bits of an orange crate licked at by the flame, and then she stands up.

Byrne and Rawson are in the front parlour, sitting in the dark. Four in the morning, the world a blue-grey shadow, they brought her the news of Freya's death. Waking her from deep sleep with a knock at her door. They have just come down from the glacier and they need coffee, a place to sit quietly, someone to talk to. They are sitting together, not speaking, waiting for her.

The water in the kettle begins to hiss. Elspeth holds her hands for a few moments above the warming iron surface of the stove, and then sits down at the unvarnished kitchen table. Freya had sat here with her one evening, not long before the climb. There was something she wanted to say, something difficult. It was the first time Elspeth had seen her hesitate before speaking her mind. And then Frank had come into the room, and Freya left soon after that, without saying it. Elspeth thinks she knows what it was Freya had been about to tell her. It was about Byrne.

In the window the blackness outside is paling to grey. Elspeth imagines the mountain will look different to her tomorrow. After three years here it has become as familiar as the wall of her own small room. Mute background.

She stands up. The kettle is boiling. In a little while the morning staff will be coming in to make breakfast for the guests. The accident will be common knowledge soon enough, on everyone's mind, but the work of the chalet will go on as it must. The room will fill with voices and light, the clang of pots and pans. Eggs will be cracked, flour and baking soda will be shaken out of tins, bacon will sizzle. The cooks will quickly forget to be solemn, they will chatter and joke with one another. It will become a noisy, human room. But for now it is still involved in the night.

Years later, when she remembers Freya's death she will see everything as if contained in this dark room.

22

At the end of the summer, Rawson brings Byrne two photographs, the remnants of Freya's film cartridge. The rest of the exposures were spoiled when the camera cracked during the fall.

—I wanted to give you these, before I left. I may not be coming back to Jasper.

The ice carapace of Mount Arcturus is the main subject of the first shot, the icefield below its summit a dark amoeboid blur to one side. The clerk in the camera shop explained to Hal that the glare of sunlight on the snow caused this effect.

23

Byrne's portrait also survived the fall. He finds himself
frozen inside it. Her gift to him.

Grey peaked hat. Knee-length, weather-stained
mackintosh over a dark flannel shirt. Tinted spectacles
on a leather strap around his neck. Knee breeches,
puttees, overshoes mottled with damp. Waterproof
railway gauntlets in one hand, calfskin notebook in
the other.

Prematurely white hair, thin white beard lining
a long, bony face. Eyes look slightly Asiatic. Squint
caused by sun glare on the spring snow at his feet.
Chiselled lines at the corners of his eyes, alongside his
thin-lipped mouth.

The markings of time. The ice has been at work
here too.

24

Nineteen-fourteen. Britain and its dominions go to
war against the German Empire.

Elspeth watches Byrne come down the path to
the glasshouse in his shirtsleeves, hatless, grim-faced.
His last day of the season.

—I can't believe how quickly the temperature
has dropped this year. One day all the streams are

rushing, and the next everything's frozen over and silent.

Elspeth smiles.

—I seem to remember my father saying something like that on one of his birthdays.

She has knit Byrne a green wool pullover. He tries it on in the parlour, holds out his arms and turns to let her admire her work.

—It's warm, he says. Thank you.

That night he packs the pullover in his valise to take with him to London. He will wear it against the English damp, and take it with him to the war, to where Rawson has already gone. He will be wearing it one day on a village street in France. Past him will file another seemingly endless procession of faces, the soldiers, this time most of them chalk-white, the eyes looking away into some place more distant and unspeakable than the depths of a glacier. He will write about this moment in a letter to her, one that he decides not to send but keeps tucked in the back of his notebook.

Four years will go by before they see each other again.

25

Trask's son is kept busy in his father's gift shop. There are more people than ever coming into the park these days, despite the fact of a war. Trask has an explanation for this.

—The sad fact is that when somebody falls to their death in the mountains, like poor Miss Becker, all the fools in the world come running to see if they can accomplish the same thing.

A customer mentions the new flying machines, built to make war in the skies. Jim Trask follows the man out into the street and stares up at the peaks, livid in the rose light of sunset. To be able to soar to those heights.

He leaves home one day, unexpectedly, setting a short note and the bulk of his savings on the shop counter. This distant war has occurred at the opportune moment.

26

People talk of the war as though it is rumbling up the valley toward them. They imagine Jasper as the last bastion of the British Empire, defended in the final hour against the armoured Huns. Dynamiting the cliffs at Disaster Point to build a wall of rock rubble where townsfolk would patrol and keep watch fires.

The ambrosia of English poetry, Shakespeare, Milton, Pope, Tennyson, is recited every Saturday evening at the town hall as a tonic.

In 1916, German soldiers arrive in Jasper, shackled and locked up in freight cars. The idea is that little surveillance will be needed in a place where there is nothing to escape to. Given the choice, any sane man would stay behind the fences and barbed wire.

Much of the old settlement is still intact, half-submerged in the willow scrub. Some of the salvageable buildings are renovated, to serve as the nucleus of a prisoner of war camp.

That winter the German prisoners build a palace of ice blocks on Connaught Drive, for the annual February carnival. The blocks are cut from the frozen Athabasca, hauled up by sledge to the town, chiselled into shape and sprayed with water to cement them in place. The plan is to build a scaled-down ice replica of the Taj Mahal.

Given the tools and the material, this proves to be beyond the engineering skill of the prisoners. Instead they build a four-sided castle with battlements.

It is to this castle, lit from within by torches, that The Ice Princess, chosen by the Chamber of Commerce, will come at the end of her horse-drawn carriage procession through the town. The problem will be to keep the Princess from freezing in the thin silk costume they have designed for her.

A patriotic fever of naming soon fills up the blank spaces on the map of Jasper National Park. Battlefields. Commanders. Dead heroes. La Montagne de la Grande Traverse is renamed in honour of Edith Cavell, an English nurse at a Red Cross hospital in Brussels, tried and shot by the Germans for helping wounded Allied soldiers escape into Holland. Trask unveils the plaque at the base of the mountain.

In memory of those valiant young men and women who have gone on ahead of us to the Elysian fields.

28

Jim Trask returns to his father after three years, from a ruined world, a future of destruction.

Byrne is on the same train. He understands something more about the ice as a time machine when he sees Jim in his Royal Flying Corps uniform, direct from the Great War, having flown not over mountain passes and hidden valleys, but fortified towns, broken bridges, smoking fields.

From the east coast Byrne passed through a sequence of crowds on his way back to Jasper. An unsettled time. Soldiers, families, young women. Children travelling alone. He brushed past giddy revellers and tearful reunions. But there were just as many faces numb with grief and shock. Bodies bent around wounds. The train stations seemed to him like the waiting rooms of overcrowded hospitals. And as he came west, the numbers of people milling about the station platforms dwindled. The train began to empty.

He approaches Jasper in a wintry dawn, alone in the lounge car. It seems to him the train is sliding towards the icy edge of the world. With himself and the young man, Trask's son, its only passengers.

The young man rides into town in the refrigerator car of the train, resting on a sawdust-covered block of ice carved from the terminus of Arcturus glacier. Around the block of ice are bags of freezing salt. Led by the local pipe band, the bearers carry the boy from the train, up the street past his father's gift shop, to Father Buckler's new stone church on Turret Street, and past it to the cemetery.

❄

Elspeth

When Ned Byrne came back to Jasper after the war,
I was still at the Empress Hotel in Victoria.

The Grand Trunk had gone bankrupt, and the
chalet was all but boarded up for three years. The staff
found work where they could, or if they could. I was
lucky. I knew what was coming, and so I wrote to my
friend in Victoria, the woman I had met on the train
that first brought me to Jasper. She knew the manager
at the Empress, and helped me get an interview. Three
weeks later I left Jasper. At the time I didn't think I
would be coming back.

The war ended, and the next spring a letter came
from Frank Trask. He told me about Jim, and how he
and his wife had considered leaving Jasper and moving
back east. But now he was working again. The chalet
was his, he'd bought out his partners. He was thinking
about adding a new wing. An auto road from town was
just about finished. Now he needed someone to manage

the chalet, someone who knew it as well as he did. He was willing to offer a share in ownership, but I was going to have to give him an answer soon. I wrote back and told him I'd think it over, and get back to him within a week.

Ned had written to me as well, a few months earlier. He was living in Jasper now, year-round. He still saw a few patients in town, but as he admitted to me in one of his letters, he was really there as an amateur glaciologist. That's what he'd called himself once, the summer he left for the war, and I'd laughed. Glaciologist. I'd never heard the word before. I'd never considered there might be others like him, scientists who studied only glaciers. I thought he was the one man on earth who bothered that much with them, that this science was his alone, that he had invented it. Arcturology. The science of being distant, and receding a little every year.

I remembered a freak blizzard one evening in July, when Ned showed up for one of his therapeutic baths, despite the weather, and sat in the pool up to his neck, letting the snow pile up on the top of his head like an absurd crown.

And another evening, not long after Freya's death. Spreading a fresh white cloth over the dining room table. For him. Setting out two places of the chalet's best china, two crystal goblets, port wine, sherry, and a carafe of Frank's glacier water, with the labelled bottle beside it. I thought that would make him smile, since he knew as

well as I did that Frank went no further than the creek
for it. But I thought the arrangement still needed something more. Something he would appreciate. So I went
out to the glasshouse and cut a handful of lilies and put
them in a blue vase on the table. He came in, sat down
at the table, looked at the lilies, and then started talking
about his long lost botanical collection. The orchids and
other rare flowers that he had hoped to take back to
England with him, that would've earned him a place at
the Royal Botanical Garden. And then he went on about
the high alpine wildflowers and lichens that grew amid
the bare rock. Within an apparent desert of water, soil,
shelter, the resilient life that will find the merest sliver
of sunlight, and bloom. And I listened, because I always
listened. When he was finished his lecture, I took the
vase off the table, went into the kitchen and dumped the
flowers in the dustbin. He came in after me.

What are you doing? he said.

I dropped the vase on the floor and it smashed.
He just stood there and stared. I was embarrassed now,
I bent down and started picking up the pieces of the vase.
And then he laughed, that maddening laugh that said
Excuse me, but I just walked in the door. I'm afraid
I have no idea what's happening here.

Once more he was pretending not to see, to feel.
Or maybe not really feeling anything other than just
dismay at the fuss and bother I was causing him. As if
he hadn't shown me his kind nature, never shown me he

could laugh and feel pain and be something other than a shell.

Freya would've laughed at me if she'd seen this. I'm not like her. I don't know why people expect me to be, but they do. Perhaps it's nothing more than the colour of my hair. But I'm not full of fire. I'm not a woman out of a myth, like Freya or Sara, I don't have that kind of power over anyone and I wouldn't like it if I did. I spent my winters here, in this snowy valley, waiting for the return of this man. I was faithful. I'd had to conserve my fuel.

I stood up and said, come here. He came closer, wrinkling his brows, not sure what this was leading to, and neither was I. Closer, I said. All right, he said. He moved closer, with this perplexed grin on his face, and I reached out my hand, slowly. At first I intended to simply touch his face, I'm not sure why, to see if it was as cold as his voice, I suppose. Then I hit him. Pretty hard, on the side of the face. Slap. I knew it was ridiculous the moment I did it. He went red. He walked out of the room, and then he turned around and came back, and then walked out again. He couldn't speak. And it was suddenly so funny. Right then he looked, I don't know, like Charlie Chaplin. Walking out, coming back, walking out again.

When a week had gone by I sent Frank a telegram. "Your new manager will be arriving at the end of June."

When I stepped off the train in Jasper, Ned was there to meet me. He had changed in some way. I had always thought he looked older than he really was, but that was no longer true. When he spoke I heard for the first time the voice that belonged with that weathered face and white hair.

He kissed me and said, You look a bit sunburned.

This was a time when people understood the world would never be the same. You could be forgiven for desiring a little joy in your life. For seeking comfort in familiar rituals. People wanted to make some kind of gesture, something momentous and hopeful. There were a lot of sudden marriages.

The question was there between us for those first few days. Unspoken, but there in the embarrassed silences, the way we avoided being alone together. But after a few days it seemed we'd resisted the fever. And now we could be ourselves again. I suppose neither of us felt very comfortable with grand gestures. ❊

TERMINUS

THE TERMINUS OF THE GLACIER IS AN INSTRUCTIVE

PLACE. CEASELESSLY CHANGING, AND YET ALWAYS THE

SAME, LIKE THE SEASHORE. ICE STREAMS BECOMING

RIVERS, MOUNTAINS WEARING DOWN INTO VALLEYS.

THE TRANSITION ZONE BETWEEN TWO WORLDS.

1

Nineteen-nineteen. A photograph of the era:

A black bear, chained to a post at the golf course. Sir Harry Lauder, on a visit to Jasper, poses with Arthur the Bear. Within the photograph's frame the placid fairway runs level behind them, bordered by a neat row of pines. Trask, who arranged this tableau, is visible as a truncated arm and hat brim to one side.

Sir Harry, in straw hat and tweed golf togs, leans on his pitching wedge and eyes Arthur askance. The beloved singer is well aware of the comic incongruity. He knows just what pose to strike for the camera.

Arthur stands upright on his hind legs, the chain taut behind him. He holds his front paws out, as if reaching for the man beside him. His small black eyes are barely visible in the photograph. He does not know that his image is being captured, frozen onto film, and perhaps for that reason he looks a little blurred, as though his innocence of the camera keeps him slightly out of focus.

It is difficult, if not impossible, to cross the gap, to say what his awkward straining posture conveys. No human emotion seems quite adequate to describe the gesture of the animal.

2

Freya first returned to Hal as water.

He was huddled with others in the doorway of a trench dugout. A morning in late winter. He had been sleeping and was nudged awake by the voices of the men around him.

He remembered where he was and tried to pull the shreds of his unfinished dream around him like a blanket. It was no use. He was awake again, stiff and sore, his head clogged by a cold that has worn him down for days. The men were moving around him. Another day beginning. Someone stumbled over his leg. *Are you dead, Rawson? Let's go.*

He looked up, and saw a row of icicles hanging from the beam above the entrance to the dugout. Beads of water budding at the tips, glittering in the sun as they broke free.

I sometimes have the feeling the ice is alive.

He reached up, broke off one of the icicles and held it to his dry, cracked lips.

3

In the dream, Hal climbs down from the summit where she left him and crosses the penitent snow, her landscape.

Hal.

She is there by the ice lake, sitting on a blanket, a picnic basket beside her. Cutting into an orange with her pocketknife. Hal steps from the snow onto the ice, sheds his jacket and sits down beside her. She hands him a slice of orange. The day is warm, aegean. They stretch out together on the blanket, under a turquoise heaven, and laugh about his fears. They kiss.

Now they are together on the long train east.

Newlyweds. They will live in his father's riverside cabin. He will write and she will travel, he would not keep her from that great passion. She will make excursions to the mountains of Wales, to the Lake District, and come home with tales of storms sweeping across the dark waters of Windermere.

He wakes and knows the dream is wrong. A betrayal of her fire, the spirit that rushed through him and was gone. He remembers an evening in her room at the chalet.

—About that city, Alexandria the Farthest. You said there was a legend.

She was sitting cross-legged on the bed, a map unfolded in front of her.

—Yes. The locals say their ancestors were the only people who defeated Alexander the Great. And they did it without drawing a sword. The story went something like this. When he arrived in the region with his army, Alexander was forced to call a halt. There was a slight problem, you see, his soldiers no longer wanted to fight. It was discovered that during their victorious march across Asia, the army had collected a huge city of tents in its wake. A city of refugees, people whose cities were burned, escaped slaves. Wandering merchants, confidence artists, prostitutes. And a few travel writers, too, no doubt. Rootless people, pulled into the wake of this great thundering mass of armoured men. And when

Alexander's soldiers discovered this, they couldn't believe their luck. They'd never stayed more than a few days in any one spot, and here was this maze of tents and pavilions travelling along with them, a place to go drinking, to hear fantastic tales from other lands, to dance and make love. Discipline in the ranks all of a sudden went to pieces.

—Hard to believe.

She laughed.

—That's what Alexander thought. His goal of world conquest was so close. Aristotle had told him India was at the edge of the earth and he was almost there. So he sent out a proclamation, demanding that these camp-followers pack up their things and go home, for the good of the army and the empire. But it did no good. Next he tried attacking the tent city and burning it, but as his advisors pointed out, sacking one city of refugees would only end up creating another, and the problem would begin all over again. In the end he had to set his army on a forced march through a desert, promising the men plunder such as they had never seen when they reached India. Well, after a few days of this relentless pace, the tent city lagged behind and was left to its fate in the middle of a wasteland.

—And this became the city of Chojend.

—Eventually. The story goes that they wandered the desert for a few years, like the Israelites.

Until their momentum ran out, I guess. Although they say some of their number kept on moving, searching for Alexander's army, and were lost to history. That's the millennial part of the legend: the hope that the wanderers will come home some day.

—So what brought you there?

She began to roll up the map.

—The name, of course. *The Farthest.*

4

Hal Rawson returns to Jasper from the Great War, from the battles of Ypres, the taking of the ridged salient at Passchendaele. He works for Trask again as a guide. Watching the jaded tourist ponies plodding down the loop trail to the stable, he thinks: that is how I ended up back here. Sleepwalking.

He meets Byrne from time to time at the chalet, but always finds some excuse to avoid talking with him. When their eyes meet he looks away. The doctor is the one man in this town who would know what the past four years have been for him. Or what he may have missed. He imagines those four years of ordinary life as a single morning. A holiday. Getting up early to make a sleepy child's breakfast. Talking with his wife, whose face he cannot see. Saying whatever it is husbands and wives say to each other.

He feels ashamed in front of Byrne, like a boy trying to mimic the speech and walk of a grown man.

He wakes often from nightmares. There are complaints from some of the tourists he takes on packtrips about his screams in the night.

An English watercolourist is his last client. He calls Hal his *equerry* and talks with him about the great English poets.

They camp at night below the Ancient Wall, a sawtooth ridge that cuts black into the powder of stars.

The watercolourist tells him of the Austrian painter, Wilhelm Streit, who passed through the Athabasca valley in 1857, on a tour arranged by George Simpson, governor of the Hudson's Bay Company. Simpson commissioned several paintings for the company headquarters at Lachine, Quebec. To reveal to guests the glories of the fur empire he commanded.

—I read Streit's published journal before I embarked on this trip, the watercolourist says. To compare my reactions to his.

Streit did not like the way the wood burned in this country. He thought it snapped harshly, with a disturbing echo. He did not like the way the rivers flowed. And the trees were thin, scabbed, spaced too far apart.

He travelled in a canoe with the company

traders and clerks. He camped with them, ate with them, slept in tents with them. And while they hunted, he set up his easel and sketched. He could not work in anyone's presence. He needed solitude.

The party went over Athabasca Pass and down the Columbia River to the Pacific coast. A message from the artist was sent back overland to Simpson. It despaired of

. . . the problems of light. . . . I stare helplessly at the blank canvas . . . qualities I cannot render in paint. . . .

He sat surrounded by the debris of his craft: paints, brushes, rags, jars. Staring out the window at the grey sky. Waiting for the frozen river to flow.

The governor's reply, reaching Streit at his winter quarters in Victoria, was a single sentence.

You will render them in paint.

Streit, in desperation, fell back on European principles of the picturesque. He tore up his field sketches, used them as fuel to heat his damp, drafty room, and painted, from nostalgic memory, the Austrian Alps.

The watercolourist asks about Hal's poetry. Why hasn't he published another volume? There are those, Brooke, Sassoon, who have written of the war.

—War is not a subject now, Hal answers. It's a form.

—I suppose I'm committing the same error as Streit, the artist says, but somehow I feel that this landscape is very English. Nothing like our green fields and hedgerows, I know. But when I look at these mountains, these roaring rivers, I fancy I can see England as Blake saw it, with his visionary eye, and for some reason that thought makes my hair stand on end. What do you think, am I being ridiculous?

—I don't know, Hal says. I've heard there's a cave entrance somewhere at the base of Mount Arcturus. The National Geographic expedition found it a few years ago. If you go in far enough, they say, there are places where you can reach into crevices in the rock and touch glacial ice. You're actually *under* the icefield. A thousand feet of ice over your head.

The painter leans forward.

—And. . . ?

Hal shrugs.

—And that's all it is. Ice.

5

Eight local men haul a Wing and Sons piano up a lower spur of Mount Arcturus, to the col known as the Stone Witch. Rawson is one of them. The avant-garde composer Michel Barnaud has arrived in Jasper in 1920 to give the one and only performance of his "Mountain Impromptu." Barnaud's New York patrons have paid them well to ensure that both composer and piano reach their destination intact. A reporter from the magazine *DisChord* is also on hand to record the event.

From the ridge there is a vertical drop of over seven hundred feet into Avernus chasm.

Barnaud wrote the piece without a definite ending. As he tells the reporter, it is finished when he decides it is finished. He plays for twenty-seven minutes, bent over the keys with his eyes closed as if in pain, then with the help of the carriers he pushes the piano over the lip of rock into the chasm.

There is a brief crescendo of torrential chords as the Wing and Sons tumbles end over end, followed by the splintering of wood and a swiftly diminishing rumble. The composer leans forward and watches without visible emotion as the shattered carcass of the piano slithers out of sight into the trees on the valley floor, trailing dust and tangled wire.

When informed that the site of his composition was also that of a recent climbing casualty, Barnaud is delighted. That night, townspeople with torches search the floor of the chasm, looking to salvage some of the valuable materials from the wreckage.

Ivory keys are found later in the summer by hikers, alongside the Avernus trail. Often they are mistaken for the teeth of mammoths.

6

As he does every year, Hal's father sends him a new book. This year it is a novel he unwraps from the brown parcel paper, *The Age of Innocence*.

Before he reads it Hal tears out every second page.

7

Elspeth finds him in the stable at dawn, brushing a grey gelding.

—This can't go on, Hal.

—I know.

—So what are you going to do?

Hal lifts a bridle from its peg on the door post. The horse lowers its head and he slips the bit into its mouth, pulls the headstall over its ears. The horse tosses its head and Hal strokes its neck.

—I'm going for a ride.

8

At Byrne's shelter he climbs from the saddle, drops the lead rope. The horse shifts its weight and leans its head down to sniff halfheartedly at the snow. Hal looks at the horse's flank, dark with sweat, and turns away.

The door of the shelter is open, a half moon ridge of blown snow on the floor. He stumbles in from bright sunlight, his blind forward grope halted by the back wall. His blistered fingers find the curling edges of two photographs, tacked to the beam above the fireplace. Freya's portrait of Byrne, and the blurred shot of Mount Arcturus and the icefield.

Hal searches the room, finds an empty tin water pail and takes it outside with him. He climbs up above the shelter, onto the nunatak, and fills the pail at a place where a thin rivulet of water spills over a shelf of rock. He carries the pail down to the horse and then goes back inside the shelter.

He crouches in front of the fireplace, digs in the ashes and builds a pyre of half-burnt sticks. He searches the shelf for matches, then the table, where he finds one of Byrne's notebooks. He drops into the chair, claws through the pages of the notebook with numb fingers, and stops when a word catches his eye. *Freya.*

The entry is dated the day after her death. A matter-of-fact description of the events of the night before. Only one phrase cracks the smooth clinical surface of the prose: *poor Rawson. . . .*

Underneath the entry, a paragraph in quotation marks:

"The growth of an individual life is always attended with the following sequence: generation of heat; a rhythm in time which establishes an equilibrium of varying duration; an end which produces a glacial cold. I do not think that I am reaching conclusions that the facts will not support, by a conjecture that with the cycles of life on earth things happened in the same manner."

Louis Agassiz, 1837

Hal thumbs back through several pages. Nature observations, temperature measurements. The dates run backwards to the beginning of summer, apparently without any other mention of her. Hal sets the book back on the table, gets up from the chair and crouches again in front of the fireplace, rubbing his arms.

Byrne enters, bangs against the door in his haste. Hal stands up.

—Doctor. I was hoping you'd be here.

Byrne stabs a finger out the doorway.

—Your horse. Its hooves are down to the quick.

He sees something in Hal's eyes, looks away.

—I followed the blood on the ice.

Hal nods.

—I've probably ruined the poor beast.

—That's very likely.

—There's ice like crushed glass up there. Wearing boots you don't realize it.

—*Up there?*

—Yes. I took the horse across the icefield. The guides have been saying somebody should try it, for years, but no one did. Perhaps they were too much in awe of the place.

Byrne rubs a hand through his hair, down the back of his neck.

—You were up on the névé, with the horse?

Hal nods.

—A partial traverse. From the Saskatchewan glacier to the Arcturus. About fourteen miles.

—Then you must have . . . you came down the icefall.

Rawson lifts a fluttering hand.

—On the winged steed of inspiration.

When he lowers his hand it is still shaking.

Byrne breathes out slowly, pulls the chair out from the table.

—Please, have a seat. Or lie down on the bed. You should rest. Then I'll help you get the horse back to the chalet.

Hal sits down again on the floor, draws his knees up and rubs his legs.

—I prefer this, thanks.

—You should've started a fire, Byrne says with forced lightness. Made yourself some tea.

—I couldn't find any matches.

Byrne turns to him, feels his coat pockets.

—I forgot. That's my fault. I hid them. Otherwise the climbers that stop here use them up and I go without heat all night.

—That wouldn't do.

—No.

Byrne rubs his hands together.

—I'll boil some water.

Hal watches Byrne's movements sleepily.

—I see I'm not the only intruder on your glacier these days.

—Oh, you mean Trask's machines. The road's not finished. They haven't actually been on the ice yet. I'm hoping I can keep it that way.

—I doubt you'll have much success butting heads with Frank.

—We'll see.

Byrne glances over his shoulder. Hal is staring at the floor.

—The icefield, Byrne says. Tell me why you did it.

Hal shakes his head.

—I'm not sure. A lot of reasons came to mind. Then I thought I should talk to you instead.

—Why?

Hal shrugs as if the answer is obvious.

—Freya.

Byrne freezes in the act of striking a match.

—She came to see you, Hal says. Before we left for the Arcturus climb, while the club was gathered by the creek. I went to talk to her once at dawn. And she wasn't in her tent. I didn't know why, then. The perfect English gentleman had me fooled for the longest time. Good show, old boy. But the answer came to me, just the other night. I was camped below Jonah Shoulder, under a billion stars, and I had a vision.

He laughs.

—A damsel with a doctor in a vision once I saw. And I realized you were a human being after all. She got to you.

Byrne patiently nurses the fire into life. He turns to glance at Hal's shadowed face.

—So what do you want from me now?

—More of her. I want to know how she looked to you, what she said, everything you can remember.

—I didn't get to know her very well.

—It was just cold and quick, then. Like with the women we both made use of during the war.

—It was a long time ago, Hal.

—And now she's Our Lady of the Ice.

—What does that mean?

Hal stands up. He sways in the centre of the room.

—I thought she would be my muse. But I couldn't write about her. I tried, but nothing came close. I didn't have a language for something I'd never encountered before. Those carvings out there on the rocks would do a better job of describing her than I could. Battles, dreams, arrows. The sound of her voice, how could words follow the shape of that?

Hal closes his eyes. He takes a step forward and his knees buckle. Byrne catches him in his arms, eases him onto the bed.

—Tired.

Byrne holds him for a long time, until his shivering stops and he realizes Hal has fallen asleep.

9

Dusk has fallen when Byrne comes back in from examining the horse. Rawson's eyes are watching him from the corner of the darkening shelter. Byrne tells him to stay the night.

—I'll take the horse down myself and return in the morning.

Hal shakes his head.

—I've got to go back. Alone.

He has to finish this day the way it began. Outside he takes the reins and leads the horse. Byrne walks with him for a short distance without speaking.

When he is about to go on alone, Hal turns towards Byrne.

    —I'd like to talk to you again. I didn't say . . . what I wanted to say.

    —About Freya?

    —No. The war. I need to talk about it.

    —Tomorrow, in town. Come and see me tomorrow.

10

Hal descends along the edge of the lateral moraine, where the surface is more stable, leading the mute and spiritless horse. When he reaches the mounds and sinkholes of the till plain, the immense weight of stillness descends around him. He remembers an evening just like this, on the edge of a Belgian village.

    The long battle for the ridge was finally over, and for a brief time the guns went still.

    His ammunition column was given the order to move. They packed up and led forward the mules that carried the shells. The road they followed, jammed at first with columns of grey soldiers returning from the front, was soon empty, and then disappeared altogether as if swallowed by a mudslide. The only way forward to the new position was through the muck and debris of no man's land, along the edge of the ruined village. As they struggled forward, he realized that beneath their feet there had once been a cultivated field. Now it was a ghost landscape of churned muck, metallic wreckage, dark red pools. White bodies half-submerged. The men rubbed their chilled hands over anything, burst shells or crackling, unidentifiable debris, that still radiated heat.

Smoke drifted silently. Above a shattered concrete pillbox, taken from the enemy and used now as a dressing station, the red cross flag snapped, as homely a sound as laundry on a line. The distant cries of the wounded had become so familiar and unanswerable, like the chirping of birds in a city, that only later did he recall them. The world was Sunday quiet, peaceful. A peace he stepped across in terror, waiting for it to explode.

11

A week after Hal's ride across the icefield, Elspeth sends for Byrne, a message to hurry to Trask's office at the chalet. Rawson is there, looking scrubbed, rejuvenated. As if camp smoke and saddle leather have never touched him.

He surrenders himself to the doctor's care. On the way to the new hospital in Jasper he lifts his head and laughs at a sudden revelation.

—My God. The poetry I'll be able to write.

He was missing for the whole week. Byrne waited for him and he did not appear. Then he was seen walking up the road to the chalet, out of nowhere. He stepped into Trask's office, dressed in the suit he wore the day he first arrived in Jasper.

Good heavens, son, Trask said. *Are you getting married?*

Rawson stood stiffly by the door, as if afraid to cross the threshold.

I won't be able to continue in your employ, Mr. Trask. The reason, to be perfectly honest, is that I'm cracking up.

12

Elspeth:

We arrived in Edmonton last night. Hal talked a little on the journey, but now he's walled himself up.

On the train he laughed at the fact that he went to war for the most unoriginal of reasons, to forget a woman. What he didn't imagine was that this war would crush that grief under something a thousand times worse.

He wanted to be taken to the hospital. He said he was quite willing to "give himself up." I'm planning to stay with him for a few days. I'll write again when I'm coming home.

Ned

13

Byrne stands in the unlit cave of a bedroom in Jasper. Dusk. The sky outside his window is green. He dips his cupped hands in the basin of water on the table, splashes water up into his face and hair.

He has just come from Edmonton on the train. In the dusty frontier capital he could not sleep, had little interest in food. Hanging in transit between the poles of his world.

The nuns who were caring for Hal left him with Byrne. He spent hours at the hospital, until Hal finally began to tumble down a long slope of talk. It began with a chaotic dissertation on the vocabulary of war. *A mine blew a boy's legs off. That's what we called being fucked without a kiss.*

The words spilled from him, became an avalanche. Shards of a private language, names, memories from childhood. At the end of it all Hal slept. Two days later Byrne left for Jasper.

He lies down on his narrow bed, not bothering with the thin blanket. He breathes deeply, the air entering and leaving his body as if through an open window.

At dawn he hears ocean waves. The sound washes him up into consciousness. He rises stiffly, stumbles to the window, and opens the shutters. Looking for a figure veiled in white, walking away from him out of the dream that has just ended, a young woman shading her eyes against the glare of sunlight on bleached sand. A figure that changes shape as it recedes into the bright distance.

There is no ocean. A haze of smoke from tourist campfires drifts along the river. Automobiles and motorcoaches rush along the new highway, the roar of their approach and passing like the ebb and flow of waves.

He turns away from the window and sits down at the desk. He will write out his memory of the dream while he is still half-awake, before its mood and precise architecture fade in daylight.

I was alone in my old consulting room in the Strand. And then Father appeared. He wheeled in an examining table with a body on it. The corpse of a young woman. A girl, really. A thin, consumptive, almost androgynous body. The face skeletal, the skin bluish and mottled. I thought we were going to examine the corpse for probable cause of death, and so I waited for Father to begin with some kind of preliminary statement of superficial characteristics. Instead he stepped away from the body and sat down shakily in my armchair, his hands falling helplessly into his lap. He was grief-stricken, I realized, and I was expected to mourn with him. I said nothing. I didn't want to appear heartless in the face of his evident pain, but this dead body meant nothing to me.

Within the dream I decided the girl must be Freya, even though the part of me that was observing or creating this dream knew that it wasn't her. I looked at the body again and one of the arms jerked slightly. I glanced over at Father. Postmortem nervous spasms, he said. In rare cases they can be quite pronounced. I nodded, keeping my eyes on the corpse. The fingers began to twitch. I heard the intake of breath. Father kept his head bowed. A tremor passed over the corpse and then it sat up. We'll just have to wait for this to pass, Father said. The dead girl opened her eyes. She looked at me. Her face was no longer a mask of skin stretched over a skull, but had regained the warm pink glow of life. Her lips moved. She was speaking, although I could not hear the sound of her voice. She smiled, as if amused by my solemn look, and laughed, and again I could hear nothing. My father still sat in the armchair, his hands clasped together. We'll just wait, he said. It will lessen and then cease. I sat down on the sofa beside his chair and watched the girl, waiting for her reawakening body to return to its proper state of lifeless immobility. Instead, she climbed off the table and began to stroll around the room, examining the mementos and framed photographs on my shelves.

Eventually she came to the door and opened it. Sunlight poured in.

Trask perseveres in his lobbying of the park administration and the next summer he is finally allowed to go ahead with his plan for motorized snow coaches on Arcturus glacier. The first step is an access road for the snow coaches, up along the crest of the south lateral moraine to the midpoint, and down onto the ice.

The spur line from the town to the chalet was torn up for the war effort, but now the gravel highway that was begun by German prisoners-of-war has been completed, by men desperate for any paying work. Farmers, bank clerks, teachers.

Trask has saved much of the lumber from the settlement cabins. With it he builds a rustic information booth by the roadside, where motorists stop for postcards and refreshments.

Three years after the end of the war, the tourists are trickling back into the park. Trask allows himself some cautious optimism. He has heard of a new wave of explorers massing out there in the cities. Families in automobiles who will glide through the mountains on smooth gleaming highways. Checking the names of glaciers in illustrated guidebooks. Gazing in awe at a world that is no longer invisible, no longer a blank space.

The only problem now is the doctor.

—They found the poor fool lying there, froze solid on his trapline.

Frank Trask steps into the chalet barber shop, batting a folded newspaper against his leg. He scrapes his muddied shoes on the sill. Byrne is seated in the one chair, his eyes closed, while Yesterday the barber lathers on the tall tales and shaving soap.

—His friend wanted him spruced up for the funeral, so they brought him to me. Well, I tried my best, but the soap was too warm. It iced right up and stuck to his face. Congealed, you might say. In the end I had to use a hammer and chisel to get him shaved. And you know, that was one of the best damn shaves I ever gave anybody, quick or dead.

Trask watches Byrne's face emerge as the razor slices through creamy lather. He remembers the crust of ice on Byrne's beard when they hauled him out of the crevasse. With his eyes closed he looks much the same now as he did then, stretched out on the lip of the chasm.

Byrne's shave is finished. He opens his eyes.

—Good idea, Trask says. Trimming those whiskers. You were looking pretty biblical. This is much better.

—Thank you.

—Hold that chair, Yesterday. I just need a word with the doctor.

Trask follows Byrne out onto the step. He holds up the newspaper.

—I've just been reading about a fellow called James Joyce. It says here he's written a great big fictitious book that nobody can understand.

—I've never heard of him.

—Well the thing is, he's a native of Dublin, like yourself. That's why I thought you might be interested.

—What's the book called?

—*Ulysses,* but God knows why, because it's about an Irish Jew. Tell me something, why is it you Irishmen always have to complicate everything?

—What have I complicated?

—My life. I hear you've been to the warden's office about the ice-crawlers.

—That's right. I don't want them up there.

—Well, they're going up there. Parks has agreed to it. Everybody but you wants this to happen, it'll make work for a lot of people. Besides, in case you hadn't noticed, the access road is almost finished.

—I know.

—The Prince of Wales will be here in August, and things are going to be ready, goddamn it. I don't need any Irish patriots blowing up bridges.

—Frank. . . .

—Okay, that was a joke. But let me ask you,

what right do you have to complain about the road? The ice hasn't exactly been kept pristine with you squatting in your hut all these years. I really doubt you've got plumbing up there. How long will it be before your table scraps and Christ knows what else starts melting out at the terminus?

—Your men are cutting down trees near the moraine.

—That's right.

—Do you know how long those trees have been there, Frank? Hundreds of years. It's like a little Arctic up there, everything is fragile. The trees grow very slowly that close to the ice.

—And now they're in the way. Ned, in this world the trees and rocks have to move, not the men.

—That's not what you told Sara's people.

Trask laughs.

—Ned, this is the most worked up I've ever seen you get, and it's all over a row of stunted spruce. If I were you I'd get down to the chief's office right now, before you cool off again. You'll impress the hell out of him, trust me, and it may just save the rest of your trees. Good luck with that, but don't think for a minute the road's not going in. It is.

He steps back into the barbershop doorway, and then turns again to thrust the newspaper into Byrne's hands.

—Here. Catch up on the real world.

16

Byrne enters his house on Miette Street in the afternoon to find that Elspeth has been there. The curtains on the front window and in the kitchen have been opened.

He moves into a shaft of sunlight, wondering how long she waited for him, and when she left. The sun beats a molten shield onto his chest.

17

He cuts the binding strings on his old notebooks, goes over the tables and columns of data. If his calculations are right, the ice that had surrounded him in the crevasse at the end of the last century has finally made its way to the terminus.

And if he were still in the crevasse, if they had not rescued him and he remained frozen there until now, he would have travelled, in the intervening quarter of a century, a distance of slightly over half a kilometre. A distance he can traverse easily on foot in about seven minutes.

In support of his calculations, a tooth-shaped boulder that he had made note of during his ice velocity measurements is now perched on the edge of the terminal slope.

This boulder rests in the same orientation in which I first found it, further up on the ice surface, and is wholly surrounded by clean white ice, making it unlikely that the stone was ever dislodged by melting and simply rolled here.

The marking of red paint he had made on the rock has weathered away to brown flecks resembling lichens. Another three days of melt brings it tumbling down onto the till plain.

He spends each day at the terminus, prowling through the muck and slush. Nothing. The glacier cracks, crumbles, sloughs off fragments of itself.

For the first time in years he comes down with a cold and retreats to the chalet. He huddles under a blanket in a deck chair on the promenade, watching the glacier through field glasses.

The poplars in the valley snow gold. An early blizzard whites out the distinction between glacier and surrounding terrain.

Two days later he sets out for the shelter, his last trip of the season, to bring down his books and papers.

18

By the following summer, Trask's road onto the glacier is nearing completion. It has taken much longer than he expected. Park officials, engineers, geologists have been consulted at every stage. And Byrne has been a factor as well, with his warnings about destabilizing the moraine.

Trask has built a bus terminal that will house a new, larger glacier diorama, a cafeteria selling hot food and drink, and perhaps, if early profits justify the expense, water from the mineral spring can be piped in for a sauna. *For the exclusive use of those taking the guided tour onto the glacier. Towels provided free-of-charge.* For the exterior of the terminal he envisions an igloo-style façade to go along with the "little Arctic" motif of Trask's other exhibits.

A sunny pleasure dome with caves of ice!

He wonders if it might be possible to import penguins to swim in the melt pool at the terminus. Of course their wings would have to be clipped. And in winter, there could be hockey games right on the ice.

Arctic. The word, used by Byrne, has given Trask an idea for a new promotional brochure:

"Scientists tell us that the altitude and permanent snow of the Rockies has created an arctic landscape in miniature. A tundra of hardy animals, tiny flowers, never-melting ice.

"This means that you can now journey to these accessible 'polar regions' without leaving the comfort

of your automobile. See a world that only a few brave explorers have seen!"

Trask paces the deck of the chalet. He is troubled by something else Byrne once told him, the undeniable fact that the glaciers are now in a state of swift recession. Not much is lost every year, a few feet at most, but the rate could increase given the trend to warmer weather during the past few seasons. In time—centuries from now, but then again perhaps in Trask's own lifetime—there may be nothing left for visitors to see.

It seems ironic to Trask, another joke at his expense in the country of illusion. That the ice should be disappearing at the same time that someone has finally found a use for it.

19

In the afternoon he strolls down to the till plain, where the work crew is hacking out the roadway with pickaxes and spades. The men are covered head to foot in wet, grey mud. Their breath steams out in the cold air. Behind them, dark smoke rolls from a rusted metal drum.

Trask watches from his vantage point on the nearest moraine. A good place for construction, he realizes. The natural and man-made mounds of rubble blend together. Even the men look like part of the landscape. One man is crossing the till plain, carrying a bucket of chipped ice from the glacier. For the beer, Trask decides. The beer he pretends not to know about.

He looks up to see Byrne watching as well, perched on a boulder at the terminus, a rucksack on his back. Trask calls to the foreman and has the work halted.

—Call it a day, boys.

The men toss their shovels and pickaxes in the back of the stake truck and climb in after them. The truck rumbles to life and crawls slowly up the winding road to the work camp.

Trask climbs down the moraine, crosses the bridge over the meltwater stream, and waves to Byrne. He makes his way over the loose stones of the till plain towards him.

—Ned, you look like an old raven. You look like you're thinking *Now what are those strange humans up to this time?*

—What do you want, human?

—Let's take a walk, on the ice.

—I was just on my way down.

—That's too bad. I haven't done any ice-scrambling for years and I'd rather not break my neck if I can help it. Truth is I haven't set foot on the glacier since the expedition. I want to see what the tourists will see when I send them up there.

—Are you courting me, Frank?

—Fine, forget it. If you won't take me I'll go by myself. And my frozen carcass will be on your conscience.

Byrne slides down from the boulder.

—It's too late in the day to go scrambling around up there.

—You won't be overrun, Ned, that's all I wanted to tell you. The tourists will be driven out to the turnaround point, they'll be allowed to leave the vehicle and have a quick look around, ten minutes at the most. It's nowhere near this hermit's cave of yours. There aren't going to be any restaurants or lavatories or billboards on the glacier. I want these people to feel like they're going back into the ice age. It's got to be *wild*. As far as safety allows, it's in my best interest to keep this place just the way it is.

Byrne nods.

—Where's this turnaround point going to be?

20

They climb the ice slope, until the distant lower icefall rises into view.

—You can't really see the spot from here, Trask says. It'll be above the icefall, on the plateau.

Trask raises his hand, traces a serpentine pattern in the air.

—The road will come down the moraine in switchbacks, like this, and then run about halfway across the ice. We'll clear a space, like a skating rink.

He drops his hand, glances at Byrne and frowns.

—What worries me right now are the melt streams up there. According to you, they change course all the time. How are we supposed to keep track of that? If somebody fell into one he'd be gone, *whoosh*, and down a mill hole quicker than a rabbit.

—I won't be using the shelter anymore, Byrne says.

—What?

Byrne tugs at the strap of his rucksack.

—I'm bringing everything down. It's going to take a few trips.

Trask shakes his head.

—I don't know what to say to you, Ned. I never do. I guess I've been wasting my breath.

—I'm heading down now.

—Are you leaving Jasper, then?

—No. I'll still be nosing around the terminus once in a while. I'm just getting tired of the climb.

—Well, I won't hold you up. So long.

—You should stay here for a while, Frank. Look around. It's quiet. You might enjoy it.

—I might at that.

21

The sky has clouded over, and the rising wind carries spits of rain.

Trask watches Byrne make his way across the till plain below. *I'm not going to follow after him like a lost tourist.*

Instead he starts off at an angle across the ice, skirting a small crevasse, in the direction of the work site. He reaches the far edge of the glacier and picks his way down through the rubble at the base of the lateral moraine.

After a few minutes he realizes his mistake. He has entered a deepening gully of loose rock, slippery with meltwater. The gully quickly becomes a ravine. The chalet and all other familiar landmarks are hidden from view. He stops and looks around for a moment, cursing his own stupidity. *Trask's guided walking tours.* He has little choice but to scramble up the steep side of the gully. He slips twice on the way, scraping his hands and knees. Climbing out again onto the glacier, he is shocked to find himself bent double, gasping for breath, his head spinning. Too much time spent at a desk the last few years.

The sky has grown darker, and the wind is rising. A true juggernaut of a rainstorm is on its way over the mountain wall. Trask scans the till plain. The sullen red glow of the fire drum is like a beacon to him in the distance. At the drum he will at least be able to warm up before hurrying back to the chalet. He descends, his bootheels sinking in the soft ice of the terminal slope.

At the foot of the glacier he halts again to catch his breath. He hears the faint creak of ice pinnacles nudged by the wind. Around him in the waning light lie fissures and spines of congealed icy mud, wet boulders, still pools of grey water. *Well, you're right in the middle of it again.*

He leans against an upthrust pinnacle of dirty ice, on a shelf at the edge of the meltwater tarn. The first fat raindrops begin to fall around him, onto his coat, the back of his neck. The pinnacle, sculpted by water and sun, rises in a graceful curve over his head. He nestles for a moment within its scant shelter. *Just like a folded wing.*

22

Trask makes it back to the chalet in the evening. The rainstorm has drawn off to a few scattered droplets.

The sky is clearing again.

He finds Byrne sitting on the stone steps below the front entrance, his field glasses hanging around his neck.

—I thought you'd be coming right behind me.

Trask shakes his head and climbs past Byrne. At the door he pauses.

—Yeah, it's quiet up there.

In his office Trask shuts the door and hangs his wet jacket on the hook. He unlocks the corner cabinet, takes out a pony glass and a bottle of whisky, pours himself a full measure. He sits at his desk, the glass in front of him, but does not drink.

There must be an artist in the construction crew, he muses, a man who missed his true calling in life. An undiscovered Michelangelo. Most of the workers are Greek and Italian, after all. They grew up in villages with that sort of thing on every street corner. Myths. Icons. Religious to the point of mania.

All that work for nothing, as it turned out. When he reached the fire drum, he had heard behind him the familiar groan and crack of ice giving way, then a heavy splash. He had turned to see ripples spreading out across the meltwater tarn. The shelf of dirty ice along its rim had collapsed. The pinnacle was gone.

But ice floats, he thought at the time. *Where did it go?* The rock and mud clinging to the pinnacle must have weighted it down.

Trask shakes his head. The wasted effort. Didn't the fellow realize how short-lived his creation would be? He probably did. That's why the thing had been unfinished, looking as if it was just emerging from the ice.

Better stick to building roads and bridges.

He gulps down the whisky, then holds the glass at eye level, his elbow resting on the table. A framed photograph of Jim sits on his desk. He looks for a long time into the eyes of his son, and then glances up at the window. Shadows of raindrops slide down the thin curtains.

There is another possibility, he finally admits, one that instinct tells him to keep to himself. There are enough odd characters around here already. Loners, drunks, an eccentric doctor. He wouldn't care to be thought one of them. And Byrne would tell him that what he saw could easily be explained as a natural phenomenon of ice erosion. Condescending blather. No, he decides, he won't be turning this into one of his incredible tales to entertain guests at the chalet.

Trask pours himself another glass. He raises it in the air. A toast, to the anonymous artist.

23

In the new year a telegram arrives from Byrne's stepmother, telling him that his father is ill and wishes to see him. He packs a suitcase, buys his train ticket, and then rides out to the chalet in one of Trask's motorcoaches to see Elspeth. He finds her in the glasshouse. Kneeling in front of a planter, cutting roses. He tells her he is leaving the day after tomorrow.

—I'd like you to come with me. To meet Kate. And my father.

—How will you introduce me?

—This is my friend, the woman I don't see for days, who leaves flowers on my desk while I'm out. The woman who comes to my house in the middle of the night, then disappears the next morning.

She says nothing, turns back to her work. He picks up one of the tools lying on the potting table, a slender metal cone with a wooden handle.

—There's one of these in every garden and nursery I've been in, but I have no idea what it's called.

—That is a dibble.

—Not a very grand name, is it?

—It does a humble job. Making holes.

He smiles.

—It's a good thing I didn't make botany my life's work.

She sets down the garden shears and stands up, wiping her hands on the front of her apron.

—I'll go with you, she says, but I have to see to a few things around here before I can leave.

—I'll wait.

24

They return in the spring, having stayed with Kate for almost a month after the death of Byrne's father.

There are days in Jasper when all the faces Byrne sees on the street are those of strangers. He overhears scraps of conversation in languages he cannot identify. He finds windows of restaurants and gift shops inscribed with new and unfamiliar names. Old wooden shop fronts and hotel doors refurbished with bright awnings, lit with flutings of turquoise and pink neon, a novelty that the park administrators loathe. He wonders if somehow he lost his way and wandered unwittingly over an unknown pass into another town, in some more prosperous valley.

On a cool evening in April, the most disorienting sight. Sara, stepping lightly from an automobile on Connaught Drive. The Sara of a quarter century ago. A mirage, an impossibility. He approaches, heart pounding, and then she turns.

Byrne can only stare in wonder at this youthful ancient woman. Sara's daughter, Louisa. And her husband, a tall, soft-spoken man whose name Byrne forgets moments after they are introduced. The two of them have just returned from their honeymoon.

—Doctor Byrne is a friend of Mom. And Dad. One of the few who'd sit through their endless stories.

—Louisa, I'm sorry about your father. I was in

England for two months and I didn't hear about it until I got back.

Louisa's grey eyes are like Sara's. They gaze back at him without fear or scorn.

—Mom's selling the homestead. Dad asked her to. She's moving into town, and she says she's buying one of those new phonographs. She's going to sit on her porch and listen to opera.

Byrne shakes his head.

—I don't believe it.

—She's been in Edmonton closing the sale on the land. We're meeting her at the station.

—I'll go with you. I haven't seen her since last summer.

Louisa smiles.

—I remember something Mom said, when we were visiting Dad at the hospital. He was hoping to come home in the spring, and Mom said that in Jasper there used to be two sure signs that winter was over. One was the glacier lily poking up through the snow, and the other was Doctor Byrne stepping off the train.

—I never thought she'd ever go anywhere near the station. Or the town for that matter.

—Here she is now.

Byrne follows her gesturing hand. Sara is there, on the far side of the busy street. At her feet a bulging leather satchel, the one Swift had called his portfolio, in which he had kept all his important papers.

Sara waves, waiting for a slow cavalcade of automobiles to pass before she crosses. He has seen that look in her eyes before. She has something to tell them. Something that happened on her trip, a story worth sharing.

He steps into the street, propelled by the ingrained habit of courtesy, to help her across.

At that moment, dodging through the stream of traffic, he understands that her woven fabric of legend and history includes him, like a figure in a crowded tapestry. The same way he had thought of her. With her words transcribed into his notebook, he had set her aside as he would a museum artifact. One facet of a design he hoped to complete when his long vigil came to an end.

Now he sees himself as a character in a story told to her daughter, and perhaps some day to her grandchildren. *The doctor, Edward Byrne. The one who fell into a crevasse.* He wonders how the story she tells them, the one he is moving through now, will end.

25

Watched Elspeth yesterday in the glasshouse, her hands delving and turning in rich, dark earth. She says she would never use a fork or trowel for this task. While I always seem to have something in my hand, a tongue

depressor, a magnifying glass, a stick. Something to hold
between me and the cold, wet hide of the world.

She never asks about the glacier, about whether
I'm still keeping on with the vigil. Sometimes I think I've
come around to her way of thinking on the matter, but a
twenty-five year habit isn't easy to break. Right now I can
hear the sound of water running outside my window. The
snow is melting.

26

June 20, 1923. Jasper is flooded with the sun's heat, but spring warmth has scarcely touched the Arcturus valley. To travel from one region to the other on this day, one must pass a threshold of low clouds shedding ice rain. On the far side the sky clears, but the sun's heat is diminished.

This year Byrne is a guest at the opening ceremony of the Glacier Tour. He had agreed to act as an advisor during the trial run three days before, so that none of Trask's machines, or their important passengers, would end up at the bottom of a crevasse. Now that the road and the turnaround point are ready, Trask has invited him to be the first person to step from an ice-crawler onto Arcturus glacier.

Elspeth sees him off for the day on the chalet steps.

—You weren't invited? he asks.

—I'm sure the idea never entered Frank's head. He probably considered having me stand here, waving a silk handkerchief, while he and the boys rode off into glory.

—And here you are.

—Yes, but I only came out to ask a favour.

She holds out her hand. In her palm sits a green, egg-shaped stone.

—Yesterday a little boy brought me this. He was hiking around on the till plain with his father all day. Tourists from New York. You should've seen the look on that boy's face. He thought all the world's treasures were out there, and he wanted to share them with me.

—You're not going to keep it?

She nods towards the other side of the valley.

—That's where it belongs. For all the other boys to find.

27

Trask is present to welcome everyone, townsfolk, tourists, visiting dignitaries. He stands before the freshly-painted wooden gates of the bus terminal, conscious of the panorama of snowy mountains that forms the backdrop to his speech of welcome.

The cavalcade makes its progress from the bus terminal beside the chalet to the staging area in plush new motorcoaches. Byrne sits next to a Japanese alpinist, the leader of the upcoming expedition to remote Mount Alberta. The story in town has it that the Japanese team plans to leave a silver ice axe at the summit, in honour of their emperor. Stitched into the high collar of the alpinist's coat is a tiny silver crest, the stylized image of a creature Byrne cannot identify.

The rocking of the motorcoach as it crawls across the till plain makes the two men bump shoulders. They turn and smile at one another.

The alpinist introduces himself with brisk formality.

—Allow me to break the ice, as you say in English.

His name is Kagami. His hand, when Byrne clasps it in a brief handshake, is warm and dry. He understands that the doctor is an expert on the glaciers of the region.

—I myself, he says quietly, have a keen interest in glacial dynamics. Perhaps too keen. I once spent a night in a crevasse, on the Mer de Glace of Mont Blanc. Purely out of scientific curiosity.

He smiles, adjusts the glasses on his nose.

—A foolish thing to do.

Byrne nods in agreement, and then, after a moment, asks,

—So what was it like? In the crevasse.

—Cold, Kagami says.

To his own surprise, Byrne laughs.

—Cold, Kagami says again, and Byrne wonders if any humour was intended in the reply. Kagami seems to be searching for words.

—There was a thunderstorm that night, he says after a long moment. The ice lit up, blinded me. When it was dark again I thought of my family. It seemed as if I could hear their voices, far in the distance. This was the way I would leave them. Cold and alone.

The conversation has fallen into an unexpected chasm. Byrne searches for a bridge.

—The symbol on your collar. What does it represent?

—This is Ryu, the dragon. The emblem of our mountaineering society. And a good luck charm.

—Why is that?

—The dragon has power over clouds and rain. In winter it hides in a dark blue lake, and on the first day of spring it ascends to heaven.

The motorcoach stops with a jolt. They have arrived at the terminus, where Trask has built a concrete platform for his ice-crawlers. The guests step off the bus dreamily. Lulled in the cradle of the machine.

The wind buffets them awake. Jacket collars are pulled up and gloves slipped on. Men who have neglected to wear any extra clothing stroll about casually in their shirt sleeves, hoping to appear unimpressed by the biting wind. Others gather together, grinning and making jokes about the balmy weather, caught up in the aura of adventure and at the same time embarrassed by it.

Trask's four ice-crawlers have a military look. A boxlike metal exterior, tank treads, and a sliding panel in the roof where passengers can take turns with binoculars or camera. The slogan Road to the Sky is painted in silver on the side of each vehicle. The drivers stand impassively at attention by the doors, polished enough for a parade ground inspection.

When everyone is assembled on the platform, Trask gives another speech, cautioning his guests to remain in the staging area until it is time to board. He wants everyone to understand the risks before they set out.

—First the interpreter will tell you about what you will see on the glacier, and what precautions to take if you leave the vehicle, at your own risk.

It has turned out there are not enough places on board the ice-crawlers for everyone who has been invited, and so the interpreter must deliver his lecture before the tour departs.

The nervous interpreter steps forward, steers an inquisitive boy away from the edge of the platform. He claps his hands briskly twice, blushes, and begins.

—If you'll look to the left there, above the roof of that first ice-crawler. . . .

Byrne steps off the platform and does not hear

the expected voice calling him back. It must be his drab clothes, he thinks, that camouflage him from the sharp-eyed young interpreter. He blends in with the rocks.

28

This is his first visit to the terminus this season. Most of the lower glacier is still mantled in white. Mushroom caps of snow top the boulders around him. Byrne taps his alpenstock ahead of him like an ice axe, wary of the ice crust on the rock beneath his feet.

Away from the crowd and the rattling motorcoach, he can stand motionless, hold his breath, and hear the rushing of newly released water as though it were flowing through his veins.

Despite the cool weather the braided meltwater channels are already running swift and deep. He follows one of them upstream to the edge of the tarn, then stops and anchors his alpenstock with a sturdy jab into the wet clay.

He crouches, pushes up his coat sleeve, and lowers his hand into the bone-cracking cold water.

Wavering in the reflected sky, the ghost of the moon.

He touches the rounded stones under the surface with his white, bloodless hand.

There was a seashore, he remembers, stretching out into a grey haze of distance. The young woman in the dream stepped out of his consulting room onto this shore. He had heard the cry of gulls as he woke, the sound of the waves.

Don't wade out too far, a woman's voice calls to him. He turns. She is walking toward him down the strand, dangling her white canvas shoes by their knotted laces. Her hand holding the sun hat on her head. He moves towards her across the stream.

Freya? Sara.

Behind her stretches an embankment of grey sand, broken by a flight of stone steps.

She waves to him, and he remembers. *Mother*. A day long forgotten, given to him now in its fullness. He takes his hand from the water. Turning away from the sea, from the tide slipping out on Dublin Bay, he walks towards her, blinking, into the fierce sunlight.

29

Powdery snow whirls around him in a sudden gust of wind. The riffled water of the tarn laps at his boot. He stands, shivers. There is no longer any reason for him to be here. He glances back at the staging platform. Trask is waiting.

He turns, and retraces his steps along the shore

of the tarn. He slips his wet hand into his pocket and his fingers find the stone Elspeth gave him. He takes it out, sets it down in the dark clay, and walks on.

He blinks. Something gleamed there for a moment, amid the grey rubble just ahead, catching the sun. Byrne steps forward slowly. A mote of colour appears at his feet. He crouches, leaning on his alpenstock for balance, to get a closer look.

Peeking out between the halves of a shattered stele of limestone, a tiny purple-pink flower. *Orchidaceae*. The petals tremble in the icy wind.

An exceedingly delicate and lovely flower.

Quickly he takes note of sexual characteristics, number of petals, the single ovate basal leaf. There can be no doubt. *Calypso bulbosa*. The Calypso Orchid or Venus' Slipper.

He kneels in the cold muck.

An orchid. His scientific understanding contracts. Orchids do not grow here. Nothing grows here. The unceasing collision of ice and rock grinds away all life. Nothing can survive at the terminus.

Byrne gently nudges aside shards of rock, exposes the stem of the orchid. There must be organic matter of some kind beneath the surface. His fingers probe into the cold grit flecked with splinters of ice, slide along a flat surface, a straight edge. He scrapes further and exposes a dull glint of grey metal. The dented, punctured remains of a tin specimen box.

30

When he returns to the staging area, the crowd is lining up to board the ice-crawlers. One of the guests, a man girded in a display of shiny new mountaineering garb, complete with rucksack and hob-nailed boots, asks the interpreter how long it took to pile all those rocks alongside the glacier.

—No, that's natural, the interpreter says with a patient smile. It's a lateral moraine. As I mentioned earlier, the ice did all that work.

—We're waiting for you, doctor, Trask calls.

—Sorry, Byrne says. I've decided to pass on this trip. Go ahead without me.

—Suit yourself.

Byrne steps up close to the Japanese alpinist, who is standing apart from the line of boarding guests, and touches his shoulder.

—Aren't you going on the ice-crawler?

—No. Mr. Trask invited me to the foot of the glacier, but no farther.

—Then come with me, Byrne says in a whisper, glancing at the restless crowd with its panoply of cameras. I want to show you something rather extraordinary.

❅

ACKNOWLEDGEMENTS

I would like to thank the following people for their help and encouragement: Kristjana Gunnars, Rudy Wiebe; Wendy Dawson, Liz Grieve, and Eva Radford at NeWest Press; Nana Avery, for her stories of Ireland; David Arthur, for sharing his wealth of mountain lore. A special thank you to Sharon and Mary.

Ben Gadd's *Handbook of the Canadian Rockies* (Jasper, Alta: Corax, 1987) was indispensable during the writing of this novel. Sexsmith's expedition is based on that of James Carnegie, Earl of Southesk, in 1859-60, as described in his book *Saskatchewan and the Rocky Mountains* (1875).

Other important works were: *Studies on Glaciers* by Louis Agassiz, edited and translated by Albert Carozzi, (New York: Hafner 1967); "Edward Byrne: A Life in Ice" by Yoshiro Kagami, *Journal of Alpine Exploration*, ii, 6 (1951); *Climbs and Explorations in the Canadian Rockies*, by Hugh Stutfield and J. Norman Collie, London: Longmans, Green and Co. (1903).

❄